A Week by the Sea

Lionel Bairnsfather

*for
Lucinda Jane*

Published in Great Britain 2012

HOME GUARD BOOKS
Cottingham Way
Thrapston
NN14 4PL
01832 734630

Copyright © Lionel Bairnsfather 2012

ISBN 978-0-9572120-0-8

Printed By

www.direct-pod.com

All rights are reserved. No parts of this book may be reproduced, stored on a retrieval system or transmitted in any form or by any means, electronic, mechanical, photocopying, recording or otherwise without the prior permission in writing from the publisher and copyright holder.

Contents

	Page
Prologue	i
Chapter 1	1
Chapter 2	31
Chapter 3	61
Chapter 4	85
Chapter 5	108
Chapter 6	133
Chapter 7	156
Chapter 8	187

Photographs

Fire-float *Massey Shaw*	i
Dover Marine Station	42
Men leaving Bray Dunes	125
Loading troops from the water	137

Preface

Although the story which follows the prologue is fictional, it is set against the 'fact' of Dunkirk, a name which has become synonymous in British history with the evacuation of the British Expeditionary Force in 1940 through *Operation Dynamo*, the success of which enabled Great Britain to confront alone for two years an enemy which in months conquered most of the rest of Europe.

The prologue sets out some of the key facts leading up to the operation. The story follows the events as they affected the lives of three young people, and one of the hundreds of 'small boats' that crossed the Channel to rescue men from a French beach – London Fire Brigade's fire-boat, the *Massey Shaw*.

Massey Shaw
Lionel Bairnsfather

Prologue

The British government knew it would almost certainly be involved in a war again when Germany invaded Czechoslovakia in May 1939. Only months earlier, in an attempt to prevent this invasion, the British Prime Minister, Neville Chamberlain, and the French Prime Minister, Edouard Daladier, had met the German Chancellor Adolf Hitler's demands that a portion of Czechoslovakia populated almost exclusively by a German-speaking population – the Sudetenland – be taken over by Germany (*the Munich Agreement*). In return Hitler gave the assurance that he had no further territorial ambitions in that country, or any other in Europe.

Suspicious of Germany's foreign policy intentions, British military planners in February 1937 authorised the creation of an Expeditionary Force comprising almost 400,000 men, and 100 medium and 200 light tanks. This would be shipped to the Continent at the outbreak of any war to take its place with the

Belgian, Dutch and French armies – the Allies - which together far outnumbered the German forces ranged against them in men, tanks, transport and artillery. For example, only around 10% of the German military transport was motorised leaving 90% horse-drawn, and Germany had at best 2,500 tanks to the 3,000 the French army alone could field. So was there any real reason to fear Germany's territorial ambitions? The British government hoped not as, unlike the last war in 1914, Britain would not be embarking on any military venture in 1939 from a position of strength financially, and certainly not militarily. The reasons for this are many and complicated, so suffice it to say here that Britain's Expeditionary Force had to rely on the strengths of its Allies in the cause of maintaining European peace – the leader of, and largest by far, being France. War eventually came to Britain on the 3rd of September, two days after Germany invaded Poland.

It is a matter of record that Britain with monotonous regularity neglects its armed forces until it is almost too late. The Falkland Islands Campaign in 1982, the First and Second Gulf Wars in 1991 and 2003, and most recently Afghanistan were all begun without adequate military resources. So it was in the 1930s when this level of brinkmanship was often justified by politicians with the fact that Britain had far more economic interest in its colonies overseas than on the European mainland, and sea-power was essential to protect its trade. Thus the Royal Navy then was the equal of any other two countries combined, but it was a dominant position under constant threat particularly from Germany which had begun its own naval building programme. For the British the 'arms-race' was all about ships which sucked-in essential resources from the other services. An important example was armour-plate. With the navy's insatiable appetite for this commodity, tanks for the army were of secondary importance within a limited military budget. One irony of the time was the order by the British government in November 1938 for 2,000 tons of armour-plate to be purchased from the world leader in its production – the Skoda works – in Czechoslovakia! Within months Skoda, under the country's new German leadership, would be turning-out tanks for the German army war machine.

The real fear, unstated of course in public, was the parlous state of the country's air force and how this was likely to leave Britain horribly exposed to a German bombing campaign – should one occur. Experience in the Spanish Civil War two years earlier had shown how devastating bombs were on unprotected civilians and whereas the English Channel could offer a real barrier to invasion, it could not stop German bombers from flying over it. The mantra *'the bombers will always get through'* became the driving force behind a last-minute obsession with Air Raid Precautions, and hundreds of millions of pounds were spent installing shelters, protecting buildings, and training professionals and volunteers in Civil Defence programmes from 1938. Chief among the latter was the provision of adequate medical facilities, and by the outbreak of war in September 1939, 250,000 extra beds had been prepared in hospitals and converted country homes up and down Britain to deal with the projected numbers of casualties from bombing. This level of provision extended to the medical services attached to the Expeditionary Force with a comprehensive system of Casualty Clearing Stations (CCS), Field Hospitals (BGH) and 13 Hospital trains to move wounded servicemen via 6 Hospital ships back to Britain. With the facilities went the men and women of the medical services. They performed daily miracles of care for both military and civilian casualties once the German army began its attack on the Allies on the 10th May 1940, the attack proving numbers do not necessarily guarantee success. As it drove the Allied armies back towards the west coast of France nurses dragged their wounded charges from one BGH and CCS to another, their Hospital trains often coming under attack. By the time France sued for peace on the 17th June, six Hospital trains had been destroyed or captured and three Hospital ships damaged or sunk by the German Luftwaffe.

In England the British, French and Belgian soldiers rescued from Dunkirk and the nearby beaches were landed at a number of South Coast ports with the majority at Dover and Ramsgate. Soldiers began arriving from the 25th May as first Boulogne then Calais fell to German attack. On the 26th May, *Operation Dynamo* was launched with the intention of rescuing as many allied troops as possible from the last port in their hands - Dunkirk. Initial estimates supposed that up to 50,000 might be successfully brought back. In fact, in just over a week by the time the operation ended on the 4th June, the total reached was 339,729 of whom around 181,000 were landed at Dover. Adding the 26,402 who were brought back before the operation officially started brings the total to 366,131 – 224,686 of the British Expeditionary Force including 13,053 wounded, and 141,455

Allied troops, mostly French.

The first wounded to arrive were unloaded by civilian volunteers and the military and rushed in any transport available to nearby hospitals. From the 26th two Hospital trains arrived at Dover Marine Station with a third in reserve ten miles away, and by the end of the evacuation they had moved 4,646 casualties out of the 6,880 landed who required hospital treatment.

Operation Dynamo concluded on the 4th June. However, the navy continued its rescue efforts elsewhere. Throughout the next three weeks under the code-name *Operation Aerial*, British ships lifted 191,000 troops and more than 30,000 civilians employed by the military from French ports on the Normandy coast, Cherbourg peninsula, and along the Bay of Biscay as far south as Bayonne near the border with Spain. It was while conducting these evacuations that the largest single maritime loss of life in British history occurred when the 16,000 ton liner *SS Lancastria* was bombed and sunk off St. Nazaire with the loss of over 4,500 men and women – three times more than the loss of life from the *Titanic* sinking.

These operations were a triumph of dogged determination and good planning far exceeding expectations, and saved a huge nucleus of trained men, irreplaceable in the formation of a new army which would go on eventually to win the war.

But what of the battle for France itself? Obviously it was a disaster, and the success of the Dunkirk evacuation only served to highlight the lost opportunity of victory had the British army and air force been properly provided for with armour and adequate numbers and types of aircraft. In fact *Operation Dynamo* might not have been possible at all without one British counter-attack on the 21st May south of Arras. With just sixteen Mk2 Matilda tanks, two Territorial battalions of Durham Light Infantry, and the support of a small French anti-tank unit, Major-General Harold Franklyn smashed the SS Totenkopf (Death's Head) Motorised

Infantry Division taking over 400 prisoners (who were shipped back to Britain via Dunkirk). Initially planned as part of a much larger Franco-British operation it stopped the Germans in their tracks. Shocked and worried that this might herald a far larger Allied counter-offensive, Hitler halted any further German advances for two days until satisfied it was likely to be an isolated set-back. But the two days of re-grouping forced on the German generals by their leader, and the time needed to set in motion their continued advance gave the Allies an all important breathing space, and if the French forces promised for the battle had turned-up, may even have promised much more.

Much has been written about the doubtful quality of the French army at this time, but spread all along their frontier with Germany it was inevitable that the fast-moving Germans, concentrated into two armoured columns, would pass many of them by. It is undeniable that without the bravery and sacrifice of the French forces in contact with the enemy in the north-west and in the Dunkirk perimeter, the evacuation would not have been the success it was.

The British government once again learned a lesson that one ignores one's defence at one's peril. Reliance on others to provide one's own national security is always far costlier in the long run, and no excuse can forgive the deficiencies of such poor military procurement by successive British governments throughout the 1930s. We can only speculate how different the world would be today if the British Army and Air Force had had the equipment to stop the German army and turn it back. Far too much of the eventual success of Dunkirk depended on the skill and ingenuity of the Royal Navy, and bravery and self-sacrifice not only of young, untried soldiers, but also people like Nurse Elspeth Breen, Private Jack Mason, and Fireman Simon Parson, who with the fire-boat *Massey Shaw,* found themselves spending a week by the sea..............

Chapter 1

Wearily Elspeth Breen left the sluice room. It was a nurse's nightmare and fast approaching a ward record. Six times poor Mr. Pemberton had rung for a bed pan since being admitted a little over three hours ago. What had he eaten that could possibly destroy her last shift on nights so dramatically she wondered? Probably something too old, but too tempting to throw away. There had been a growing number of others since rationing started, people taking chances with some of the strangest things in an effort to beat the system. Using liquid paraffin in baking had been the latest classic, it being until now a well known laxative until some bright spark at the Ministry of Food suggested it could be used instead of lard! Fungi that looked like mushrooms had been one of the commonest the previous autumn even before rationing started. But with only half an hour to go she managed a smile. Today, Sunday May 26th, 1940, had been circled in pencil on her calendar for almost two weeks. Two days off, then three months of working in daylight. Perhaps now she could enjoy the opportunities that moving to London had promised the day she joined St. Thomas's.

Elspeth had wanted to be useful since the age of four. Born and raised in the small village of Elton on the northern border of Northamptonshire, many hours of the school holidays were spent travelling with her father in his car visiting local farms. His profession as a veterinary surgeon opened the eyes of the young Elspeth to the magic of medicine and even years later, when the family gathered for dinner each Christmas, conversation would inevitably turn to her first dabbling in that magic. How as a child she had attempted to take the family dog's temperature with a garden thermometer. How it was the nurse's cloak, part of that year's Christmas present, which had saved her from serious injury when their Jack Russell terrier attacked the little hand so intent on insinuating six inches of copper and glass into its rear end.

After qualifying in the autumn of 1939 at Wadham Training College in Cambridge, she had moved to the main premises of St. Thomas's Hospital in London only to find that, fearful of destruction by Germany's Luftwaffe, the hospital was packing up to move out to a safer location – back to Wadham College! So she found herself once more in Cambridge. It was like that at the outbreak of the war. New rules and regulations, a plethora of official announcements, air-raid shelters springing up everywhere and trying to remember where you left your gas mask. Six months later, however, after the fear of aerial bombing had faded while Germany concentrated on occupying Poland, they had moved back. Now she was finally in London, aged 22, determined to 'do her bit' and pursue the dream of bringing her new skills to the aid of the suffering. Of course there was also the prospect of a wider circle of friends, and perhaps an opportunity for romance? To date, most of those doing the 'sufferering' she encountered as well as the men in her life had been old and frail patients, worthy causes yes, but hardly exciting and certainly not romantic. Throughout training she had devoted herself to her studies, and as the slightly 'gangly' girl matured into an attractive young woman, boyfriends and parties were increasingly forfeited in pursuit of her chosen vocation. Friends at college even considered her, albeit affectionately, as something of a 'swot'. The level-headed student reputation served her well with the tutors, but had done nothing for her social life and lately the attraction of letting her hair down occasionally had occupied her thoughts more. Unfortunately, the only eligible males within the confines of a busy hospital, the Doctors, were off-limits being too tired, timid or highly trained to warrant serious pursuit. Two week night-shifts hadn't helped either, so it was a mixed blessing when she'd been literally bowled over yesterday by a young man.

While making her way back to the hospital after running an important errand for the ward sister, a young man had collided with her in the blackout and knocked her to the pavement. Full of apologies he'd gently helped her up and with a strong arm around her waist to support her, walked her to the main entrance where, in the dim light of the foyer, she was able to see him clearly. He was tall, good-looking with dark brown eyes that reflected his concern for her and, as she recounted ad-nauseum to her friends over the next twenty-four hours, she found herself loathe to let him go. As they chatted he told her his name was Simon Parson, and that he was a fireman, one of the crew of a fire-boat on the Thames. He'd been hurrying to where it was moored temporarily at Westminster Bridge when they bumped into one another. At her prompting he described his boat, the *Massey Shaw,* so that she could watch out for it on the river, and as they were saying goodbye, her heart leapt when he shyly asked if he might see her again on her first free day. Far too enthusiastically she would tell herself later, she agreed to meet him on Monday afternoon at 3.00 o'clock, and then he was gone.

Simon had also moved to London to escape a quiet time. His home city of Oxford, that of the 'dreaming spires', held no allure for a young man who, at 24, was the youngest qualified fireman in the county. He'd even tried to join the armed forces at the outbreak of war, but his reserved occupation was considered too important by the fire-service and they refused to release him. A tip from the Station Commander in Oxford that the London Fire Service was gearing-up for war and looking for more staff offered the opportunity he needed. After two visits to be grilled by a very serious interview panel, he was accepted into their River Department, and transferred to his new job in the February.

From the first day he discovered that working the river Thames was a far cry from extinguishing the odd farm fire in the Oxfordshire countryside. The river had a dark side hidden from the casual observer. The docks which lined its banks presented an opportunity for criminal activity which was impossible to ignore for some, particularly now the country was at war. A growing 'black-market' meant Simon's crew spent more and more time attending fires which had been started to cover up the theft of food or cloth, or any of the dozens of items that had become increasingly difficult to purchase legitimately. Occasionally there would even be the sad task of helping the river police retrieve a body from the filthy water. The hours were long and, like Elspeth, Simon spent weeks working shift patterns which prevented him from enjoying the company of other young people socially. By the third week of May he was ready for a break and had decided to go to Oxford at the end of the month to see his parents. That was until he bumped into Elspeth.

Elspeth never slept well during the day. This Sunday was no different, and it was further complicated by the exhilaration that the night-shift was over at last, but there was something else. She couldn't settle and by mid-day was standing in her pyjamas looking out of her window and sipping a cup of tea. Most nurses lived next door to the hospital, but some of the nurse's quarters at St. Thomas's were situated in the upper floors of the building and offered those lucky enough to live 'at the back' an unparalleled view of London's most iconic buildings as well as the busy river. She had become used to gazing at the Houses of Parliament on the opposite bank, but today found herself scanning the river more closely. On a Sunday it was always busy with pleasure craft, mainly small launches and day-tripper ferries. It was much more interesting during the week when a different scene had become familiar. Then she could watch a myriad of working boats. Her favourites were the fat, squat tugs who bullied their way through the water pulling a string of huge barges lashed tightly together. Those travelling down river towards the docks were usually empty and would pass quite quickly. Those going the other way, however, always seemed barely able to cope, their barges, piled high with coal for the power station at Battersea, so low in the water it was a miracle to the casual observer that they floated at all. But today there was no sign of the *Massey Shaw.* She smiled and knew why she was restless.

"Get some sleep or you'll look like death tomorrow", she chided herself.

Draining her cup, she got back into bed and snuggled into the pillows, little realising that the next time she enjoyed such luxury her life would have changed for ever.

The hospital dining room was a cacophony of sound. The vaulted ceiling gathered the excited chatter of staff mixed it up then threw it down onto those sitting at the tables below. Today it was overpowering.

Elspeth had walked in on it twenty minutes earlier. She knew the room would be packed, it always was these days. Food rationing had concentrated choice in very few places in wartime Britain, and the hospital kitchen had never been more appreciated. Shouting to be heard, Elspeth enquired from her best friends, Cicely and Sarah, what the excitement was all about. Rumours were the stuff of life in the insular world of the hospital. Newspapers disappeared before one had a chance to read them, and a shortage of wireless sets and time to listen meant news was invariably second or third hand when one received it. But today the rumour was different and serious. It had begun in the usual way. A secretary had overheard a staff nurse who read a message sent to the hospital's nursing manager that revealed England might be in danger of invasion! A hundred different opinions were now swirling in the air.

The dining-room doors swung open and the noise died away as Matron entered. Behind her scurried the sparrow-like figure of the Almoner, Mr. Winslett, followed by the Chief Surgeon, Mr. Spooner. Elspeth had only seen the Chief Surgeon once before. If he was here, something important must have happened.

Once the room was silent, Matron removed a piece of paper from her pocket and unfolded it. Felicity Armor had been a matron for so long it was suspected among the hospital staff that even her family had forgotten her real name. Today her calm and imposing manner was being threatened by the news that she carried with her.

She began to read the message delivered by a Ministry courier earlier that morning.

> "Today, Sunday the 26th of May, the Minister of War has authorised the commencement of Operation Dynamo – the evacuation of our troops from the port of Dunkirk in France. I would ask you all to keep this information strictly confidential until the Ministry is able to inform the wider population in the near

> future. I trust that all of you will strive to assist those engaged in the pursuit of the struggle with Germany.
>
> God save the King."

Matron folded the paper with trembling hands and looked up. Her steady voice rang out in the hush caused by this shocking announcement,

> "Mr.Spooner would like to speak to you all".

The Chief Surgeon stepped forward and looked around the room. He barely recognised a handful of the young faces sitting expectantly before him. But his time as an army field medical-officer in the last war, only twenty five years earlier, had taught him that these young medical professionals were about to face traumatic times. Quietly he began,

> "It would appear that things have not gone well with us in France. As a hospital we have been designated a casualty clearing centre for the emergency. None of you can have any idea what that means. I can only tell

you that you will never again be so individually important. Some of you are to be sent from here to locations where you will receive casualties who have been dragged from battle and hurriedly put onto the rescue ships. Wherever possible we will deploy you in surgical teams, but it is highly likely and probable that you will find yourselves on your own at some point in a life or death situation, with little if any assistance. You may not be able to cope, but you will have to deal with that. I apologise now for sending you into this maelstrom with limited experience. However, I know you will do your best, and that is all we can ask of you. We can assure you of only one thing, you will make a difference. Please carry on, and good luck".

For a full minute the room was deathly quiet as Matron and her entourage left. Then the noise exploded in an excited roar. Cicely turned to Elspeth,

"Does that mean we lose our days off",
she shouted.

And then she felt foolish.

By 6.00 am the next morning the hospital was a hive of activity. Half a dozen cream-coloured ambulances were running a shuttle service to other hospitals in the London area emptying St. Thomas's ready for its new role. Elspeth smiled as she saw old Mr. Pemberton being wheeled out, a bedpan clutched to the blanket covering his chest. She hadn't slept again. The twenty nurses of her set had been summoned to the dining room at 10.00 o'clock the evening before. They were split into four groups, and Elspeth, Cicely and Sarah had been joined by Angela and Jane. Their first job was bagging and labelling the patients' personal belongings under the watchful eye of the Almoner ready for the move the next day. This kept them busy until midnight after which they were despatched to the hospital stores where a junior doctor, Dr. Herbert Flowers, handed them each a list of items to pack into a dozen large fibre cases. At some point in the early hours of the morning Matron arrived pushing a trolley laden with tea, sandwiches and fruit cake. Their stunned silence was greeted by a rare smile as Matron instructed them to,

"Tuck in, girls. Well done".

After she left, Cicely summed-up the occasion by observing,

> "A smile? From Matron? Things don't get much more serious than this – they couldn't!"

With their tasks finished by 5.00 o'clock in the morning, the girls left wearily to try and rest. Elspeth decided to clear her head and made her way to the hospital entrance to sit on the edge of the raised flower bed just outside. She had become comfortable with her own company during the long days studying at Wadham, and often took a short stroll along the embankment after a night on the wards. The city was waking and she watched a bus pulling up the slight rise in Lambeth Palace Road at the front of the hospital. A couple of workmen cycled past, one of them whistling as he gave her a wave. The first pair of ambulances pulled onto the hospital forecourt, the drivers nodding to her as they went inside to report. They were followed minutes later by an army lorry.

Before it had even stopped, four young soldiers leapt from the canvas covered rear, their hob-nailed boots cracking on the road as they laughed and started towards the hospital entrance. The lorry squealed to a stop, the passenger door already opening, and an older man wearing Sergeant's stripes stepped out quickly and hurried after them.

"Hold up you lot!" he barked.

One of the young soldiers rounded on him replying cheekily,

"Hush, Sarge. This is a hospital".

Grinning, they waited for him to catch up, then followed him to where Elspeth was sitting. She felt herself begin to blush as the Sergeant enquired of her,

"Excuse me, miss, Night Porter's office?"
She stammered and blushed harder as, from behind him, the cheeky soldier gave her a broad wink.

"Through the door, and to the right".

"Thank you, miss", he replied.

Then to the soldiers,

"Come on, there's work to do".

As they entered the hospital, Elspeth smiled. Another handsome man, she thought to herself, things are looking up.

After a few fitful hours of sleep in her room, Elspeth had joined the rest of the staff again, this time in one of the hospital's old lecture halls. St. Thomas's status as a teaching hospital had bequeathed it three such halls. As they sat there, the staff could hear workmen already dismantling the tiered seats from the one next door in preparation for its conversion to a clinical ward, and this urgent work had instilled in some a feeling of anxiety, but in most a sense of excited anticipation. The Chief Medical Officer, Mr. Dawson, began reading the names of the surgical and casualty teams. Elspeth's team was joined by John Traynor, a kitchen porter, and headed by Dr. Marcus Harvey, a second-year Junior Doctor. They were to operate as a first-line casualty team, and with two others would be travelling to Dover. The surgical team of older, more qualified staff would go to the general hospital at Ramsgate. Leaving London would be a new experience for most of the staff and Matron, realising this, had brought their anticipation of a seaside trip down to earth. As Mr. Dawson finished she took over.

> "There will be no opportunity to paddle or build sandcastles."

A murmur of polite laughter rippled around the staff at this rare flash of matronly humour only to subside quickly as she went on,

> "You people going to Dover will help other teams from another hospital staff a special hospital train, on which there

are minimal washing facilities. So make the most of the next few hours. It is now 12.30. Dinner will be served straight after this meeting, and you must all be ready to leave by 2.30. Not much time. You should take adequate personal belongings to last for five or six days, but please, only one small suitcase. And don't forget your gas masks!"

She looked around the room and her tone changed.

"Be professional, be patient and make us proud. God bless you".

The meeting broke up with groups of nurses chattering as they made their way to the dining hall. Mr. Dawson gathered the doctors as they left and ushered them off to his office for their last instructions. It was at this moment that Elspeth remembered Simon. With a shock she realised how much she was going to miss her date with this handsome young man. She decided to write a note and leave it with the hall porter. Hopefully Simon would have the sense to enquire about her when she failed to meet him as arranged.

Little Johnny Traynor, proved his worth the moment their coach pulled up outside Victoria Railway Station. As the rest of the staff began leaving the coach he rushed off only to appear moments later pulling an enormous trolley assisted by one of the station porters. The two of them busied themselves piling the suitcases onto the trolley and set off for Platform 5 followed by the staff who, dressed in freshly laundered uniforms and capes, drew many an inquisitive glance from the other travellers.

Elspeth was astonished at the number of people there. Apart from civilians there were hundreds of servicemen, some hurrying to or from a train, but the majority sitting or standing in groups laughing and chatting as they waited. A particularly large group of around fifty Royal Navy sailors waiting for a train to Portsmouth had staked their claim to one of the refreshment kiosks on the concourse, and began whistling and calling out to the nurses as they passed. Cicely evoked a roar of appreciation when, with a grin, she began an extravagant wiggle of the hips. The good-natured banter was infectious, and the girls ran a gauntlet of cheering, smiling servicemen all intent on outdoing the group before them. The noise gradually receded as they followed the trolley of suitcases through the barrier and onto the platform.

There were two trains parked one behind the other on the same line stretching off into the distance. The nearest one was a normal suburban commuter train, but the second in front of it was very different. The malachite green coaches were emblazoned with enormous red crosses on their sides. Standing beside the first train was Mr. Spooner with an army officer and a railway official. The group slowed to a stop and John and the railway porter helped the girls destined for Ramsgate retrieve their suitcases from the trolley. Mr. Spooner called the doctors to him and, after a brief discussion with them turned to the nurses.

"Good to see you have all made it thus far. This train will take the group to Ramsgate. As you can see, the one in front is the hospital train for Dover. Nurses from our sister hospital, Guys, will be arriving soon with their matron, Mrs. Pepper. She will take over the nursing staff on the train, which means you. I know you won't let me down, but I feel I should point out that Mrs. Pepper is a good friend of our own matron, so fore-warned is fore-armed, eh? Well ladies, once again good luck and we will see you when our job is done".

John and the porter started hauling their trolley on down the platform towards the second train leaving the surgical team for Ramsgate to wave their friends goodbye. Elspeth clutched Sarah's arm as a sudden thrill ran through her. They passed the engine of the first train and approached the hospital carriages of the second. Elspeth spotted a few of the fibre boxes they had packed in the early hours of the morning sitting on the platform, and the trolley pulled up next to them just as four young soldiers stepped onto the platform from the train. Elspeth recognised them straight away. She also recognised the voice of the Sergeant as he bellowed from inside,

"We haven't got all day.."

His voice tailed off as his head appeared at the open door and he saw the group of doctors and nurses arrive, then he started issuing his orders again,

"Right, get those boxes on first, then give these young ladies and gentlemen a hand!"

The fibre boxes disappeared with the soldiers into the carriage as the nurses gathered round the trolley to claim their suitcases. Elspeth spotted hers on top, but as she lifted her arm towards it a voice behind her said quietly,

"Here you are, sweetheart. Allow me".

The arm of the cheeky soldier from that morning reached past hers and grasped the handle. She turned slightly and looked straight into his eyes, inches from her own. The blush exploded on her cheeks as he smiled at her, something not lost on Cicely who was watching intently.

"Hey, handsome, what about mine?" she called out.

The soldier spoke without taking his eyes off Elspeth's.

"Only one at a time, beautiful, that's what I say, and me and your friend here is old mates".

With Elspeth's case in one hand, he took her by the arm and walked her to the carriage door. For a moment all eyes were on them, including the Sergeant's. There was a momentary silence followed by his roar from behind the trolley,

"Mason! You put that young lady down!"

At this everyone started laughing which allowed the soldier to help Elspeth into the carriage and place the case at her feet. He straightened up and asked,

"See you when you get back?"

"Yes, thank you", she blurted.

Quickly picking up her case, she dashed into the carriage where the blacked-out windows hid her embarrassment from those outside. She found herself smiling, but the sudden warm feeling she felt disappeared as, from behind her, Cicely declared,

"You're a dark horse and no mistake!"

Commuters were beginning their evening rush onto platforms as the engine pulled the train gently out of the station exactly on time at 5.30. In the hour before, the Guy's Hospital group had arrived and everyone set to unpacking cases, making beds, and stowing away surgical equipment and stores. The train itself was equipped as its name implied with most of what would be found in any small country cottage hospital. The first carriage behind the engine housed the boiler and the hospital porters' accommodation. This suited John Traynor down to the ground. An avid train-spotter, the nearer he was to the engine, the better. He was in heaven and had told everyone who would listen that the engine pulling the train was a 4-4-0, School's Class 5 called King's Canterbury. He even knew where and when it was built,

> "At the Eastleigh Works in 1935," he informed them enthusiastically.

Within half an hour of arriving he was on first name terms with the driver and fireman, and could confidently assure everyone that there would be no bumping and jarring on the trip – the driver was one of the best Southern Railways had. He had even elicited a promise from the fireman that at some point in the week he would be allowed to ride on the footplate.

The next four carriages were made up into bedded wards. The beds were arranged in bunk fashion, two high and ran the length of both sides of each carriage. Carriage six was for casualties who could sit, seven held the operating theatre, pharmacy and medical store, and eight was fitted-out as a kitchen and dining car. Carriage nine was curtained off into small bays for the doctor's accommodation. The next two were for nursing staff, and the twelfth and last carriage was the brake and general storage van. It was a small but efficient self-contained system of dealing with casualties which had been invaluable in France in the First World War saving thousands of wounded then, and able to speed them on their way to more traditional hospitals.

At 6.00 o'clock as the train sped out of the built-up areas of London and into the countryside, the St. Thomas's nurses sat down to their tea. They had been put into the last accommodation carriage next to the brake van. Things had been so hectic that they hadn't had much chance to chat to their opposite numbers from Guys, but the general consensus was that they were a 'good bunch'. The decision by the Guy's matron to allow them first sitting at tea had also gone down well. Cicely had been miffed at first that in the pecking order, established by her as the distance from the dining carriage, St. Thomas's being the last of the accommodation carriages were bottom. However, Sarah soon pointed out that this meant nobody, except the guard, was going to be wandering through their bedroom, at least until they reached Dover. They couldn't know that casualty numbers would eventually make the concept of personal space meaningless.

King's Canterbury steamed through Maidstone East station at 6.30 pm. Many passengers on the platforms acknowledged the significance of the red crosses on the carriages, some by clapping, others by lifting their caps. All over Britain people had been following the unfolding drama in France. A special radio appeal by the government for volunteers to take-up arms if necessary to repel an enemy invasion should it occur had seen a flood of men answer the call. Veterans of wars fought at the turn of the century mingled with schoolboys at police stations across the country, eager to join the Local Defence Volunteers as they were called, soon to become the Home Guard. The passengers on Maidstone's platforms knew where the train was heading. Anxiously they had read the daily reports of the German advances across France towards the English Channel, and the latest news that the British Expeditionary Force had 'fallen back' to Dunkirk brought real fear into the lives of all, particularly those living in this part of South East England.

Elspeth had seen this spontaneous reaction of people in the station while she peered out of the small window aperture next to her bunk. The main windows in the carriages were blacked-out, but the small inward opening section at the top afforded the upper-bunk dwellers some fresh air and a narrow view of the world outside as they raced towards the South Coast. She had headed for the accommodation carriage as soon as tea had ended to try and rest if not actually sleep for an hour. She was exhausted. Then her thoughts turned to the cheeky soldier. Two good-looking men in as many days! She smiled, and wondered what Simon was doing and whether or not he had received her note.

Chapter 2

After arranging to meet Elspeth, Simon decided not to go to Oxford after their date, but work his days-off instead. He told himself he could do with the extra money, particularly now he might have someone to spend it on. But there was also a niggling feeling since the announcement of the problems in France that he ought to hang around, for what he wasn't sure. Perhaps it was fate that this pretty blonde girl had come into his life, but then – disappointment. He'd just read the note again. Folding it quietly he looked up at his landlady, Mrs .Proctor, sitting in her armchair on the other side of the fireplace. She was knitting, absentmindedly looking beyond the needles as they turned out the fifty-something balaclava she had made in the past six months. Like the others it was destined for an anonymous soldier or sailor serving 'somewhere cold' as she would tell him when she finished each one. They had retired to the tiny front room after tea to listen to the evening news on the wireless. It was the usual non-committal announcement of the Allies 'holding ground' or 'falling back to stronger positions', and Simon felt a rising anger and sense of frustration. Why was he forced to sit here, when he could have been fighting alongside others of his age in France? As if sensing his misery, Mrs. Proctor looked up and smiled at him quickly before the hypnotic clicking of the needles engrossed her once more.

He was lucky to have found her. The little terraced house in Ashton Street, Poplar, was a short bus ride from Limehouse next to the West India Dock where the fire-boat was now based. It was scrupulously clean, she looked after his ration books better than he ever could, and they had the house to themselves. Both her husband and son were away in the merchant navy and she said she only took him on because he could speak well and was 'in boats'. With a wry smile he'd reminded her that a fire-boat on the Thames was hardly the same as a ship on an Arctic convoy, but she persisted. To her he was a type of sailor, and that was good enough.

Many of the neighbours were overcrowded, often squeezing up to five or six children as well as the parents into the narrow little 'two-up, two-down' terraced houses. A lot of the children had drifted back home from the country after their parents decided that, because the promised bombs from German aeroplanes hadn't materialised, the evacuation in the previous September had been a waste of everybody's time. The East End schools filled up once more, and now the children were everywhere. When on night shift, Simon usually waited until mid-morning before going to bed. That gave him six hours of peace, although he had soon become used to the noise of their playing. After a few weeks he noticed that they occupied clearly defined areas outdoors, and it was for this reason that Mrs. Proctor had considerately put him into the back bedroom of the little house. Unless they needed the space for a long skipping rope, the girls kept mainly to the backyards and connecting alleyways. The boys on the other hand laid claim to the street at the front of the houses. He'd gradually become aware how this arrangement had developed, and who controlled it. The girls could be trusted to play carefully and quietly under the lines of washing which regularly adorned their territory. Here they would sit in pairs or small groups discussing important girl issues, and debating the mysteries of life safe from the attention of any strangers in their remote and protected world. The boys, however, with the requirement of space for games such as football, cricket or British-bulldog, monopolised the street where, coincidentally, they could be constantly monitored and, where necessary, admonished by any of the mothers. Unless it was raining, in a street of fifty houses there would always be at least two mothers chatting on a front step, eyes never still as they surveyed the activity. On Sundays during nice weather most of them would appear, seeking the sunny side of the street and carrying a chair to sit and gossip until a meal time or child's attention dragged them back inside. And it worked extremely well. The street had evolved into a huge, outdoor crèche, with all of the mothers controlling any of the children by common consent. This enforced sense of community had been a little claustrophobic and intrusive at first, but with the world spiralling down into war and uncertainty, Simon had begun to find it comforting.

Music from the Palm Court Orchestra on the wireless filled the room and Simon closed his eyes and thought back to that morning. The shift finished at eight after which he usually breakfasted at the canteen in the dock. Sometimes, as this morning, he would then go for a short walk to watch the ships unloading. It had been an unusually quiet night, almost as if the news that Britain was now seriously in trouble had finally got through, even to the criminals in society. There had been no swindle or concealment fires, and the river police were only called out once, and that was a suspected suicide. The rest of the time when they weren't attending to small jobs on the boat they sat and played cards or read. Their control had kept them up to date throughout the night on the disaster unfolding in France, and every radio bulletin was listened-to in silence, then discussed in detail until the next. Each was more depressing than the last. Amongst the crew there had been an underlying feeling of embarrassment that other fit young men across the Channel were not having such a comfortable time. But throughout it all, Simon was also excited at the prospect of taking Elspeth out. He thought they might catch a film at the Carousel in Lambeth, then maybe stop for a coffee afterwards.

When he'd turned the corner into Ashton Street a little after 10 o'clock that morning, it had been a surprise to find it completely empty. The children would be at school he knew but, strangely, there was nobody sweeping the road outside a house, or scrubbing a step. Letting himself in he spotted the note on the front room table.

> "*Simon, we have gone to the Civil Defence meeting to see what they want us to do. They are talking about evacuating the children again. Your dinner is in the oven as I won't be back until later. Light the gas when you're ready on mark 4 for an hour or so. I'll have mine at the meeting in the Citadel, so eat it all up. Ma.*"

He smiled. It was her idea to call her Ma, less formal and quicker, she said, than Mrs. Proctor. He'd walked through the front room to the scullery and opened the gas oven. A bowl of minced beef topped off with mashed potato and greens, Ma's bubble-and-squeak, sat on the top shelf. The built-in copper in the corner of the room was lit with small wisps of steam escaping from the lid, so he knew the water had been left on for him. Great, he thought. If Ma was out he could have a good strip wash in the scullery sink before going to meet Elspeth. That would save him a visit to the Council Slipper Baths in Browell's Lane, and the threepence it cost for a bath. Whistling he'd climbed the narrow stairs to collect his wash kit from his room. He felt good. This was his first date since arriving in London three months ago, and to find such a lovely looking girl not spoken for. Perhaps my luck is changing after all, he'd thought to himself.

The bus dropped him off outside the hospital right on time at 3 o'clock and he'd walked to the flower bed she said she would meet him next to just as a military ambulance swept into the unloading area to join two more already parked there. He watched as the driver reversed his ambulance next to the others and hurriedly jumped out. Two trolleys clattered out of the hospital entrance each pushed by two soldiers. A doctor in a white coat and carrying a bag followed them as they moved to the rear of the ambulance whose doors had been swung open by the driver. Simon had felt the urge to offer to help, but in moments two wounded men on stretchers had been loaded onto the trolleys and were being wheeled carefully back into the hospital. Two more men in uniform, who despite heavy bandaging were able to walk, followed, one being assisted by the doctor. With his charges gone, the driver closed the doors then ran to the front and climbed into the cab. The engine started and the ambulance whined its way out of the hospital grounds.

He wondered what was going on. Why were the army here? Why the casualties? An accident at one of the London garrisons perhaps? For ten minutes he'd mulled over the likely causes. Deciding something had happened to delay Elspeth and the two might be connected he'd made his way into the hospital to find out. The nurse in reception suggested enquiring at the hall porter's office and in a few minutes he was on his way out clutching Elspeth's note just as two more military ambulances pulled-up. He'd walked to the bus stop and opened the note which read,

"Dear Simon, I'm sorry I won't be able to see you this afternoon. You will have heard that our soldiers are stuck in France, and we are being sent to help. I don't mean to France, just to Dover where there are a lot of wounded men coming off the ships. The authorities aren't telling people how bad things really are just yet, so can you not say anything to anyone. We should be back by next weekend sometime, when I hope we can meet up.

Yours faithfully,

Elspeth".

A twinge of jealousy made him frown. A slip of a girl could get involved, but he wasn't able to. Not only that, he'd really been looking forward to her company. It was not a good way to start a relationship. Kicking the bus stop post he'd stuffed the note into his pocket.

At a little after 7 o'clock in the evening the

train reached its destination, Dover Marine Station. This sat adjacent to the harbour and consisted of four long platforms inside the station building with three lines of track between the building and the quay. Two large cranes used for loading ships ran on the track nearest the sea, leaving two lines for parking trains in the open. The hospital carriages were pulled slowly onto one of these, then King's Canterbury was uncoupled and driven to the end of the line where a connecting section allowed it to cross over to one of the lines which ran inside the building. The points were set and King's Canterbury reversed through the building and out of the main entrance to a turntable. Here it sat steaming while a small shunting engine moved in to pull the Porter's and Ward carriages off the front of the train and transfer them to the other end behind the Guard's van. The turntable motors whirred into action turning the hundred tons of locomotive 180 degrees. Now facing out of the port, King's Canterbury reversed once more through two sets of cross-over points to arrive gently at the re-positioned ward carriages. Men scurried between the engine and first carriage, connecting steam hoses and the giant coupling link, and the train was now ready to travel back to London with casualties when required to.

Dover Marine Station

Elspeth missed all this. She was fast asleep along with most of the St. Thomas's nurses. The first shift through that night would be manned by the nurses from Guys. They had not spent the previous night working and were already busy inside the train laying-out dressings and loading instruments into autoclaves in preparation for their first patients. One person who had not missed the manoeuvrings of the engine, though, was John. He disappeared as soon as the train halted, and was in the engine's cab throughout the operation soaking up an experience he would recount for the rest of his life.

Elspeth woke with a start. For a moment she lay wondering where she was. Then the high-pitched noise which had roused her went off again, a 'whooping' sound which climbed in short bursts. She struggled with her blanket and let down the small vent window. The noise of voices and the clatter of boots and clinking metal rushed in, but she could see nothing in the darkness outside. Kicking off the covers and swinging her legs out of the top bunk she dropped to the floor and found the box of matches and small candle placed at the foot of their pair of bunks the previous afternoon for just such an eventuality. As the candle flame grew there was a banging on the outside of the carriage and a gruff voice shouted,

> "You're showing a light. Shut that window!"

Scrambling back into her bunk she pushed the window shut. Sarah In the bottom bunk, woken by the struggles above, enquired sleepily,

> "What's up, Els?"

Elspeth dropped back onto the floor and knelt next to her.

> "I don't know, but it sounds like there's a lot happening outside".

At that, the banshee whooping started again making them both jump.

> "I've heard that before!" said Sarah, "on the Pathe News. It's a boat, a big one, Cruiser or something".
>
> "No, it's a destroyer! I know 'cause my Archie's in them. So can we go back to sleep, you two?" grumbled a voice from further up the carriage.

Elspeth made a face at Sarah before turning to where the voice had come from,

"Sorry", Elspeth replied in a stage-whisper, then more quietly to Sarah, "I don't know why I'm whispering, that thing's enough to wake the dead".

"Shall we have a look?" said Sarah.

They made their way quietly to the entrance door at the end of the carriage. Blowing out the candle, Sarah let down the blacked-out window on its leather strap, and they both peered out. Sarah let out a breathless,

"Jesus wept!"

There was just enough moonlight to illuminate a scene of manic activity. The harbour was crammed with ships as far as they could see. They were tied to the dockside, then to each other in rows disappearing into the darkness. The lighter night sky was a tangle of shapes - funnels, guns, masts and rigging, overlaying one another. As their eyes adjusted to the dark they could see that this whole jumbled mass was connected to the quay by a line of gangplanks which disappeared out of sight down onto the decks of the ships tied to it. A steady stream of soldiers climbed the gangplanks to step onto the quay and safety. Military and civilian police ushered them along and, singly or in groups, they walked off into the darkness in the direction of the hospital train's engine. Occasionally there would be a pause on one gangplank, then a group of soldiers would appear struggling with a stretcher. Once ashore they were met by one of the doctor's from the train. Elspeth and Sarah had no idea who the doctors were. White-coated figures, they moved like ghosts in the dark. Elspeth craned out of the window to see further along the quay. As she did so she caught a glimpse of a group of Guy's nurses waiting by the operating theatre carriage. Parked next to them with their rear doors wide open were three military ambulances. Then a shout went up. Elspeth looked to where the shout had come from. A doctor was working on somebody on the ground surrounded by a group of soldiers. One of the nurses ran across from the train. There was a brief pause as the doctor spoke to her then the soldiers in the group bent down and picked up their friend on a stretcher. They hurried to the train following the nurse. A dull light spilled from the carriage and was reflected back from the faces of the soldiers gathered in front of it. Elspeth and Sarah watched as the stretcher was lifted into the open carriage door and taken in by someone on the train. The light vanished as the door was closed and the stretcher bearers drifted off to join the flow. Two more wounded men, each with an arm in a sling, and a third with a bandaged head walked to the row of ambulances accompanied by a civilian policeman. Another, supported by his friends, hopped across the quay behind them.

    For ten minutes the girls watched hundreds of men come ashore, some carrying their weapons, some not. Some laughed and joked, obviously relieved to be home and safe, others walked quietly. In that time, the ambulances drove off full to be replaced by others every couple of minutes, and three men were taken aboard the train for emergency surgical treatment. Then the whooping noise started again, just three ascending calls, but chilling to hear given the scene that the girls were looking at. It came from somewhere out in the night. This time they were able to pin-point the source. Sarah whispered,

"Look! Out there, those flashing lights!"
Elspeth watched them. Short bursts of light flickering from the harbour entrance. Then more, only this time from somewhere nearer the land.

"I think that's morse, isn't it?" Elspeth said.

"The ships must be talking to each other", said Sarah quietly.

She changed the subject,

"Should we go and see if the others need a hand?"

"I don't think we should start getting in their way", said Elspeth, "We ought to wait until they call us, and I'm sure matron will if we're needed".

Sarah pulled herself back into the carriage.

> "Well I'm for my bed then. No point in wasting valuable snoring time, not if it's our turn tonight".

Elspeth took one more look around then pulled the window up with the strap shutting the noise outside.

Simon and the rest of his watch had reported at first light and spent Tuesday morning on a training exercise with the new recruits to the Auxiliary Fire Service. Knowing the vulnerability of the docks in the event of a bombing campaign, the government had increased the number of fire-boats on the Thames from three to thirteen. The extra ten were crewed by Auxiliary firemen, Auxies as they were known, and training this amount of new people had become a pressing priority. Two of the new boats were based at Cherry Garden Pier on the southern bank of the river at Bermondsey and they would now take over the *Massey Shaw*'s duties. Tonight Simon and his boat would be going out on a roving patrol of the docks all the way to Tilbury. The plan was that they would be on hand if German navy surface raiders followed up their army's success and attacked British shipping or shore establishments in the estuary. It wasn't much nearer the enemy, but it was something. And Simon needed something. Again they had heard reports from control of how while he was sitting with Ma reading Elspeth's note, British ships had evacuated around 17,000 soldiers and brought them back to England. He wanted to be part of that.

In Dover, Tuesday morning was cloudy. The St. Thomas's nurses had been woken at six, squabbling light-heartedly among themselves for access to the two small washroom-cum-toilets which served the whole carriage. By seven they were dressed and ready for breakfast after which they would take over from the Guys nurses at eight. As they made their way chattering and laughing into the adjoining carriage to get to the dining car, they began to realise what the night had brought for their colleagues. One of the Guys nurses was lying in her bunk being tended by a friend who smiled wryly at them as they passed. In answer to their questioning glances she shrugged and told them,

"She fainted, poor soul".

Another nurse was fast asleep, sitting propped-up on her bunk, her ashen features a sign of total exhaustion. Sarah nudged Elspeth and nodded towards the girl's foot which dangled over the edge of the bunk. Stuck to her shoe was a bloodied pad of lint which Elspeth carefully removed and placed in a bin. They moved down the carriage, quietly now, passing two more nurses fully clothed and asleep on their bunks where they had dropped sometime in the night or early morning. The next carriage was empty. There was no sign of the doctors. Cicely turned to them with raised eyebrows.

> "I thought we'd at least catch Dr. Harvey in his pants", she joked.

But the rest of the girls ignored this quip which, under normal circumstances, would have raised a ribald discussion about junior doctors' underwear. Somebody at the back of the group remarked,

"It's like the Marie Celeste!"

They entered the dining car and began to settle at the tables. John Traynor and another porter from St. Thomas's, Billy Rich, were already there tucking into scrambled eggs on toast. Cicely, Sarah and Elspeth joined them. While Sarah went to collect their breakfasts, they began questioning John.

"OK. So what's happened?" said Cicely.

"Bloody tinned egg again", replied John.

At the rate he was eating it would appear that the egg powder had improved considerably.

"No, not the egg, the doings last night".

John paused for a second before answering,

> "Strangest thing, never seen nothing like it, but then nobody has, have they?"

They waited while he chewed. Sarah returned

with the breakfasts and sat down. Still John mulled over the events of the past twenty-four hours in his mind. Cicely, growing impatient took a deep breath, but before she could launch into him, he began to tell them what he had pieced together. He had scurried around making new friends and gleaning information from the moment they had arrived in Dover, so they knew because it came from him it was probably as near the truth as it could be.

Through mouthfuls of egg he recounted how the first evacuated troops began arriving at Dover on the Sunday morning, and by Monday the total was around seven thousand, mainly carried aboard the cross-Channel ferries. The majority of these soldiers had been drivers, mechanics and other trades who'd made their way to Dunkirk over the past week. Most of the fighting troops were still facing the German armies holding them back to allow the evacuation to build, except for their wounded who had started to return with the others. Throughout the previous night, thousands of these others had disembarked and rushed onto the trains, which were kept steaming in the main station building. Some dry clothing was handed out where available along with a mug of tea and a sandwich and, when full, the loaded trains each carrying around a thousand soldiers would leave Dover on their way to Paddock Wood station, the stop before Tonbridge. Here the WVS, Red Cross and local volunteers had set up a feeding station. The trains stopped for half an hour in a siding while the troops were fed, then continued their journey to Redhill where they changed for Guildford and eventually Basingstoke and Salisbury and various other destinations in the West Country.

The girls exchanged glances as he finished and Elspeth looked at him with a new sense of wonderment. How had he been able to find all this out? She concluded he was wasted as a porter, he ought to be a spy. He on the other hand seemed oblivious to his innate skill. There was only one thing on his mind at that moment and that was the trophy he had received from a guard on a returning train. With a flourish and a grin he pulled a blue bowl and spoon from out of his smock pocket and plonked them on the table.

> "Bet you can't guess what they are", he said.

> "A blue bowl and spoon?" Cicely ventured slowly, barely hiding her sarcasm.

John's grin disappeared.

> "Yes, of course they are, but guess where they're from. Pick 'em up, go on".

Sarah obliged, then looked puzzled as she turned the bowl over and tapped its base with the spoon.

> "They're light", she said.

> "That's 'cos they're plastic".

John held on to the word plastic, his grin back.

> "That's what a few of the blokes are getting up at Paddock. Good ain't they? Ministry of Food supplied 'em, but there aren't many of these, they're

mostly using paper and cardboard."
He retrieved the bowl and spoon from Sarah and went on,

> "After they've eaten, the soldiers are told to throw all their used stuff and paper out the window. When they're gone a team of people clean it all up before the next train pulls in. Amazing 'aint it?"

They agreed with him, it was amazing. The whole organisation was amazing, even down to these new, lightweight bowls and spoons. Then while John returned his treasured bowl and spoon to his pocket, Cicely pushed her egg around on the plate and wondered aloud,

> "But then, if they're so amazing, how have they managed to make yellow egg so grey?"

When they had finished breakfast and cleared the dishes the nurses sat gossiping for a few minutes until Matron entered from the surgical carriage. She stood for a moment until she had their attention, then gave them a weary smile,

"Good morning ladies, and gentlemen". The girls and porters murmured a greeting and sat expectantly while Matron turned the pages in a notebook she was carrying.

"We've had a busy night. I don't know if you were told why we are sitting here in a hospital train in Dover, but it has turned out to be a very prudent decision. We will be staying here, but in order not to overload the local hospitals wounded men from France have already been taken in a second train to London. I believe the first of those started turning up at your hospital on Sunday afternoon after you had left. They are continuing to use local hospitals for general medical, but we are the emergency reserve, you might say. Last night the doctors performed three operations here on the train, and those patients are in post-op care in carriage one awaiting removal to hospital. There are four other young men in carriage two recovering from hypothermia. However, we do expect things to get much busier through the coming days. I will now appoint you to your duties so that the other shift can get some well-earned rest".

Later, the St. Thomas's girls would agree that, by not referring to the Guys nurses as her nurses but as the other shift, matron was definitely impartial and a 'good egg', unlike the breakfast, as Cicely was quick to point out.

Elspeth found it satisfying to be doing general medical duties again after so long on a geriatric teaching ward at St. Thomas's. All of the surgical patients on the train were amputees, one young soldier having lost both legs and an arm to crush injuries when a house fell on him in Dunkirk. How he had survived the shock and trauma of embarkation and transport over twenty hours nobody knew. But having got this far, none of the nurses on the train were going to allow him to give up. Three of the hypothermia cases were transferred to a hospital in Ashford by ambulance just after midday, and it was at about this time that the first large ships from France entered the harbour on the St. Thomas's shift.

Sarah and Elspeth had been amazed when they had awoken that morning to find the harbour almost empty. The activity witnessed in the night seemed like a dream now that daylight revealed an empty sea. The only evidence of the previous night were three coal trucks piled high with discarded kit which were towed away noisily by a small fat shunting engine, which John missed, much to his annoyance. Four ambulances arrived mid-morning, their drivers leaving their charges parked to go and sit on the quay smoking and throwing stones into the water. With the doctors resting in their quarters, and few patients to watch over, Cicely suggested they climb down to join the ambulance drivers. It was while they were discussing it that the 'whooping' started again. This time they could see it, the creature that sounded as though it was dying. One of John's porter friends had pointed it out earlier that morning. He said it was a 'guard ship', an 'S' Class Destroyer, the *Shikari*. They could see its long grey shape in the distance where it sat, stationary, the odd plume of smoke coming out of one of its two funnels. The sound which answered it was not a shriek, but something they had all heard before in the London docks, the low rumbling of a ship's horn, a ferry was returning. They watched it make its way through the harbour entrance and head towards them. As it got closer, they could see the decks crowded with figures. Then these figures seemed to move as one, and three cheers from hundreds of throats rang out across the water. St. Thomas's shift had begun in earnest.

Chapter 3

Simon poured water from the jug into the bowl and surveyed his face in the mirror. He had gone to bed as soon as he'd got in and slept for a few hours in the afternoon. Ma had woken him at five with her usual rattle on his door, and he could smell the chips being cooked for tea. Tuesday was a 'treat' day with Ma, and each week she liked to surprise him with something new. When he had first arrived he'd sat down to any number of exotic dishes such as scampi, spaghetti, even pate-de-fois-gras on one occasion, and steak had made an appearance too many times to be either legitimately available or affordable. With most of the neighbours employed in the docks it wasn't hard to work out where the food was coming from. The one thing he never could understand was why some families who were in-work seemed oblivious to the plight of those who weren't. There were many children at the top end of nearby Ashton Street and Bullivant

Lane who were thin and dirty. Questioning this had invoked the response that either their fathers were 'away', probably in prison, or unemployable, usually through drink. The community spirit it seemed to him had its limits, and on his way home he regularly dropped a sixpence at the end of the street where these children gathered, so they might find it and buy two penny-worth of chips and crackling from the chip shop in Woolmore Street.

They also sat down that night to fish and chips, the fish an enormous cod steak, courtesy of Ma's friend Mrs. Miller four doors up whose husband had arrived back from Grimsby two days ago with a whole fish almost three feet long and a foot wide. Mrs. Miller had kept it as cold as possible, but after 48 hours and two consecutive fish meals in the Miller household, Mrs. Proctor and four other friends were the beneficiaries of Mr. Miller's good fortune at the Lincolnshire dock. Suitably full, Simon had to rush to leave and catch the bus. Mrs. Proctor

fetched his packed lunch from the scullery and
hovered near him as he laced on his boots.

> "We had the meeting", she said at last.
>
> "Which one was that, ma?"
>
> "Yesterday, you know, the Civil Defence", she answered.

Not wishing to be rude, but itching to get to work and start patrolling the estuary, Simon put on his coat and, taking the lunch from her, moved to the front door.

> "I'm running a bit late, ma. Do you want to tell me in the morning?"
>
> "Yes, alright, only they're going to evacuate the kids again, all of them this time, and no coming back".

He paused as he opened the door, and turned to her. She was obviously worried about something.

> "Oh, when?"
>
> "Couple of week's time. June the 13th. All of them".

He wondered for a moment why this should upset her so. Her son was on a ship somewhere between America and Russia. It had been a while since he played marbles in the street,

> "That does seem a bit sudden," he agreed.
>
> "Yes, that's what we thought. I don't suppose anybody knows why, do they?"

He realised what she was after. In her eyes, and doubtless many others in the street, he was an 'official' in uniform. Only a fireman's uniform, true, but because he worked side-by-side with the police and was paid by the government, he might have been in possession of some fact to help put their minds at rest. Evacuating the children the first time was seen by the general population, and particularly people living in London, as a sensible precaution by the government. Most of them had returned though after the dangers failed to materialise. Now they were being asked to move them again - and in short order. This time the Germans were just across the Channel. This time it could be a dire necessity, and hadn't Elspeth tipped him off about how serious things were? Suddenly there was a real possibility that the country would be defeated and life would change forever. What could he say to her? The same fear had been stoking his frustration since Sunday morning when he and the rest of the country woke up to find their army in France fighting for its life.

> "Don't worry, Ma, I'll sniff around and see what I can find out".

She gave him a big smile and closed the door behind him as he strode off along the street feeling such a fraud, unable even to give this old lady some peace of mind.

The nurses were working flat out. Orders and instructions flew around the carriages as men were loaded into the operating theatre in a steady stream. When Elspeth started cutting a sailor's uniform off a mangled leg she knew that the ship this sailor belonged to had been attacked. It was evidence that getting on to a ship was only the first part of a dangerous journey back, and often the men were safer on the beach where they at least could shelter from German bombers. Men were dying in increasing numbers as ships were blown up under them by bombs or mines. The rumour went round that last night two destroyers were torpedoed and bombed and over eight hundred men drowned almost within sight of England. But still the ships kept coming. After the ferry they watched arrive had berthed and discharged its grateful passengers it steamed across the harbour to tie-up until nightfall. Conditions in Dunkirk were so bad, they were told, that only Royal Navy ships would be making the crossing from now on in daylight, and the harbour reflected this. Somebody remarked that they didn't know we had so many as their view filled-up with dozens of grey shapes with guns pointing skyward. However, the supposed ban on civilian craft travelling during the day was not always adhered to. At around 4 o'clock three small fishing boats nosed their way to the quay. The first bumped its bow against the harbour wall as it squeezed between two destroyers. Its companions formed up on its stern, and forty-odd soldiers clambered from all three onto dry land. They stood in a small group and cheered their rescuers who shoved off immediately to head out to sea again. Standing beside Elspeth watching this, John said quietly,

"Like a taxi service, 'aint they, brave sods?"

By 5 o'clock there was a queue of men waiting for ambulances, and two groups of nurses and a doctor were treating the walking wounded on the quay. Two of the porters were despatched to ask the military police to gather up any field dressings the soldiers might have brought back with them and, shortly after, a military casualty station had been assembled by returning army medical staff working in a tent made from a destroyer's awning. And still the ships kept coming.

At 7 o'clock Matron, who had been on duty constantly since London, informed the doctors that the ward carriages were full, and those in them should be sent on as soon as possible to hospital. The station had been busy all afternoon as well. A dozen trains had pulled out, their carriages bulging with tired but relieved troops heading for the food station at Paddock Wood. The station master waited for the next to leave and shut down that line while Kings Canterbury made steam ready for the manoeuvre that would enable it to pull the four ward carriages off the edge of the quay. This was accomplished in twenty minutes, and after ten more, the casualties in those carriages were off to the military hospital at Chatham. With no beds for patients, Matron set about creating some. The nurses from Guys were now up and dressed and began stripping their carriage, washing it out, and re-making their own beds with clean sheets and blankets. Their cases were moved into the St. Thomas's carriage, and from now until the engine returned, all the nurses would share the accommodation. In the event, this arrangement was made permanent as for the rest of their stay the nurses would be too busy to operate as a shift. It wasn't until after nine that Elspeth and the rest of the St. Thomas's nurses made their way to the dining car. They had eaten little since breakfast but were almost too tired to do justice to the meal of corned-beef hash, potatoes and peas that was waiting for them. All they wanted was sleep.

The *Massey Shaw*'s twin diesel engines were warm enough for the boat to cast off from the dock. Earlier, at the watch assembly, the crew had been informed that from tomorrow, Wednesday, the boat would return to its regular moorings, the pontoon next to Blackfriar's Bridge. This way it would be nearer some of the important government buildings further up-river. They would be replaced at the West India Dock by an Auxie-crewed boat. For a while the crew discussed this apparent shift in the importance of the dockland sites, but things were in such a muddle now, they agreed it wouldn't matter where they were if bombs did begin falling on London. They were joined by a pilot, Arthur Black, as they would be travelling into the estuary, and pulled out at 8 o'clock to set off across the river for the south bank and their run down to Tilbury.

The skipper, Coxswain Ralph Denny, stood behind his 'dodger', a canvas screen which protected the helmsman from some of the elements, and steered the boat as they rode the tide downriver towards the estuary. The *Massey Shaw* was not an easy boat to manage. Her eighty feet length and slightly less than fourteen feet width sat low in the water, and her shallow, flat bottom made her quite unstable in rough water. She had only ever been out of the river once, when she made the journey from where she was built in the Isle of Wight. The cabin which housed the crew and the fire-fighting equipment was low and cramped and Simon joined the rest of the crew sitting on its roof to watch the wharves and warehouses slip by. The ebbing tide was emptying the river now and stretches of mud were beginning to grow along the water's edge. The high embankment threw shadows across it as the sun dropped behind London's skyline. At Deptford his attention was drawn to an old woman who had taken up a position on the bottom of a flight of concrete steps. In front of her four small children were 'working the mud' collecting firewood. One had found an old barrel and was attempting to roll it to the steps, his little body plastered in brown slime. Towering on either side of them steel barges had settled into the river bed, their huge rudders anchored until the next high tide. He heard the pilot and coxswain laughing, and smelt the tobacco burning in Ralph's pipe. As the river arced round the Isle of Dogs he could also smell the paint and soluble oil from the dozens of factories crammed together in Millwall. It made a heady mix with the aroma of decay from the drying mud. He smiled. Ralph had a solution to everything, and a pipe full of tobacco was almost good enough to overcome this assault on a stranger's nose. There were many smells on the river. Most of the wharves served individual companies who specialised in handling one major commodity, so you could almost tell where on the river you were by the smell of wheat, coffee or rubber. However, everyone knew when they were at Millwall.

Kings Canterbury returned to Dover just after 4 o'clock on Wednesday morning with its ward carriages empty. The porters began moving the injured troops from the nurse's carriage into the more suitable accommodation. It was just in time. The number of rescued soldiers being disembarked was being measured sometimes in thousands per hour, and these were now mostly infantry, men bearing the physical and mental effects of combat mixed with no food, no sleep and little water over days of desperate fighting and marching. This massive influx inevitably led to the Port and Railway Authorities struggling to get the trains away quickly enough. More and more soldiers were crowding the quayside hampering the work of the doctors and nurses working there, and an air of hopelessness had begun to descend on the medical staff. Once again Matron rose to the occasion. Fresh from her first decent rest in days she went down on to the quay and moved among the soldiers leaving the ships until she found a detachment of Royal Engineers. Two hours after speaking to their officer they had erected a barrier around the surgical and accommodation carriages of hessian toilet-block screening material mounted on poles found in the railway stores. Now her nurses could work undisturbed by the sight of thousands of demoralised troops and their murmured tales of horror and misery. She then moved inside the train. Nurses showing signs of stress were sent to the dining carriage for a meal, then to bed to rest. She took Little John to one side to speak to him, after which he disappeared. Within the hour he was back carrying a wind-up gramophone and a bundle of records, courtesy of Hobleys department store. Soon music was drifting through the carriages, and the train guard was instructed to keep the records playing. It began to work. Nurses were heard singing along to some of the records, and there was the odd gratifying sound of laughter. Word spread and records began to turn up at the guard's van throughout the morning. There was a lull shortly after breakfast and most of the nursing staff took the opportunity to rest. The music stopped and peace descended on the quay.

Elspeth had been working with Dr. Harvey since six o'clock, checking the wounded as they left the ships. They watched the last armoured trawler pull away to move to the other side of the harbour to refuel. Behind them the noise of the station subsided, punctuated occasionally by the warning toot from a train whistle, followed by the regular puffing which accompanied its departure. Dr. Harvey lit a cigarette and walked to the edge of the quay. Elspeth watched him as he peered down at the water.

"Mr. Spooner was right", he said.

> "Sorry?" Elspeth walked to join him.
>
> "About this mess. He told us back at the hospital we'd be lucky to cope".
>
> "I think you and the other doctors have done marvellously", she countered.

He looked at her and smiled.

> "Do you?"

Elspeth hesitated. It was unusual for doctors to discuss such matters with nurses, and she wasn't sure if he had been offended at her voicing an opinion.

> "We've only had that one poor boy die, and there was nothing anyone could have done about that, don't you think?" she ventured.
>
> "I'm sure you're right", he said turning to look out towards the harbour mouth, "but there were over a score who died on the way we could have saved if we had got them sooner".
>
> "Then we would have to be on the ships", replied Elspeth.
>
> "Or at Dunkirk", he said quietly.

For a moment Elspeth wondered what matron would have to say about such an idea. Her thoughts were interrupted by the destroyer near the harbour entrance. It had begun howling out its challenge to an anonymous ship approaching from the sea.

> "We'd better warn the others and grab a brew while we can", Doctor Harvey said quickly, and they hurried back to the train.

After an uneventful patrol, the fire-boat was riding the returning tide back up-river, the sun rising over the estuary behind them promising another dry day. Some of the docks were busy already, the cranes pirouetting as they hauled nets filled with goods out of the cargo ships lining the wharves. Simon squinted at something ahead on the river. A boat was heading their way, but distant enough that he couldn't make out what type at first. His attention had been drawn to the flashing as the low sun was reflected off its wheelhouse windows. They had seen no river traffic for three hours and his turn at the wheel had been merely a matter of running the *Massey Shaw* at a couple of knots faster than the tide speed. He pulled nearer the north bank to give the oncoming vessel more space, then realised what it was. A Port of London tug was hauling something, steaming hard against the tide. Her tall funnel billowing black smoke betrayed her age, a 'coaler', one of the old and grimy workhorses without which the most modern of vessels couldn't deliver their cargoes on this busy river. Today, though, she wasn't heading off to manoeuvre some ship full of wheat or steel into a berth. She had a precious cargo of her own. A fortnight earlier, on May 14th, the Admiralty had made an order that all self-propelled boats between thirty and a hundred feet long should be registered with them. The decision to evacuate the British forces from Dunkirk had been made in secret and in the knowledge that the harbour there would be rendered unusable by the Germans very quickly. And so it had proved. It had been so comprehensively damaged that only a few ships at any one time could use it, certainly not enough to evacuate the numbers of men needing to be rescued. So the troops had been told to make their way to three beach areas, and from these, small boats would ferry them to larger vessels anchored off-shore. By the end of May hundreds of small boats had already made the perilous crossing and were attempting to fulfil this part of the plan, but the numbers evacuated had been disappointingly small. It was the decision to use a long wooden breakwater, the Eastern Mole, at Dunkirk harbour which had proved most successful. Now, however, time was fast running out and the Admiralty had requisitioned the boats on their register for one last desperate push to rescue as many men as possible before the Germans over-ran the beach defences. Some of these were now being towed down-river by the tug.

Simon called to the other firemen while

the tug drew nearer. As they reached each other, the *Massey Shaw*'s crew gave a wave which was answered by the Tug's whistle. They stood in silence as the small craft were towed past. Sixteen of them, tied together in four long lines. The firemen could see Royal Navy sailors and the odd civilian in wheelhouses. Soon all the country would see this on Pathe News and in newspapers. For now, however, it served only to increase Simon's feelings of uselessness and frustration.

The *Massey Shaw* finally tied up at Blackfriars at 6 o'clock on the Wednesday morning having passed two more tugs towing their charges down to the English Channel.

Simon rushed home to Ashton Street minutes after they docked. The Watch Commander had given him hope at last. Thankfully, Ma was out, so there wouldn't be any need to discuss her fears of yesterday before he managed to get some sleep. That was one thing the Commander had insisted on. All of his watch had to go home and sleep – there was a good chance they would be going to Dunkirk! There, he'd said it. Simon could barely believe it. They had been told that, if necessary, a crew would be drawn from volunteers sometime over the next twenty four hours. How would they choose them? Their watch were the only ones who had been in the estuary. Would that count? Was that the real reason they had been sent? The watch taking over the day shift from them would surely be too tired to go. The thoughts tumbled around Simon's head as he washed. He decided to shave now rather than when he awoke so that he could get back to Blackfriars by 3 o'clock without any last minute hitches. That was the earliest the Commander wanted to see them by. He sneaked into Ma's bedroom and borrowed her alarm clock. She wouldn't mind he knew, and with two alarm clocks he couldn't possibly oversleep. He scribbled a note asking not to be disturbed until 1.30, then tried to get some rest.

He arrived at Blackfriars five minutes early so at 3 o'clock he would be able to stroll nonchalantly onto the mooring pontoon, at least it would have been nonchalant if he hadn't had to do it with a dozen others who all had the same idea. The second shock was the presence of the Massey Shaw herself. She hadn't gone out, and the day watch were busy painting over her brass-work and anything else shiny with grey paint. Worst of all, none of them looked tired, in fact they were working flat out moving things around on the deck. It appeared as if they were about to put to sea. Perhaps headquarters were sending this crew, thought Simon. The Watch Sub-Officer Andy May was sitting in the small wooden office on the pontoon and the rumour soon spread that he was picking the crew from those who had volunteered, which meant everyone. The muttered conversations between the men tailed-off as he came out of his hut and asked,

"Does anyone know anything about compasses?"

The surge of men responding to this question started the pontoon deck rocking on its wooden supports, and it was accompanied by a gaggle of voices all affirming they knew everything about compasses.

Andy steadied himself against the wall of his hut and surveyed the group of volunteers. He spotted the boy, Charlie Shepherd, who, at fourteen came every day to earn money doing odd chores about the mooring. Andy crooked his finger towards him, and Charlie elbowed his way to the front.

> "Charlie, take the trolley and pop over to Seth's and pick up a compass, alright?"

"Yes Mr. May, right away!"

The crowd stood silently watching as Charlie took the handles of the two-wheeled goods trolley and set off briskly for Seth's Chandlery in Blackfriars.

"And be careful with it!" Andy shouted. Turning to go into his hut he muttered,

> "Compass! Did you ever hear the like?"

As he reached the door someone called out,

"Is it definitely on, then?"

Andy paused,

"Aye, it's definitely on", he said, then smiled and rubbed his hands together.

When the hut door closed, the men on the pontoon settled to wait to see who would be successful. The crew aboard the boat re-doubled their efforts to make it sea-worthy and, as far as possible, invisible to the enemy.

The list was finally pinned to the outside of the hut at half past four and the men crowded round. There were thirteen names. The station officer, two sub-officers, including Andy, four of the regular crew – and six auxiliary firemen! Almost twice the normal number of crew, and only four regulars! The grumbling rose to a crescendo as Charlie wheeled his trolley on to the pontoon. He watched in amazement as Andy, besieged in his hut by angry firemen, tried to explain the list through a partly opened window. Simon joined the other three firemen whose names had been on the list. They moved to one side, forming a little group, slightly embarrassed, but at the same time elated they were going. The station officer was going to brief them at 6 o'clock. For now, it was enough that they had been picked. Simon walked over to Charlie and took hold of one of the trolley's handles. Together they pulled the load past the hut to the boat where they heaved the compass in its heavy gimble off the trolley and onto the *Massey Shaw*'s deck. The engineer, Sam, looked up at them from the deck-well and enquired,

"Where do you want it?"

"Somewhere the Cox can see it?" guessed Simon, trying to be helpful.

With an old-fashioned look at what he took to be obvious sarcasm, Sam grunted and grumbled the compass towards the front of the boat.

Throughout the rest of the evacuation, with no time to calibrate it, it never did work properly, a fact which was to prove extremely hazardous for the boat and her crew later.

Chapter 4

Elspeth got to bed at eight that evening. She had been assisting Dr. Rogers earlier in the afternoon in an operation to remove a piece of shrapnel from a young soldier's groin. He had been injured in an attack on his rescue ship and, perversely, the shrapnel that caused his injury also saved his life. It had been plugging a hole in the femoral artery and the fountain of blood resulting from its removal on the operating table had shocked them all. The resultant mess meant closing the theatre for an hour to wash the carriage down. Once the bleeding was stopped, the patient, accompanied by Dr. Rogers, was rushed to the hospital in Dover for a transfusion and Elspeth was sent to the stationmaster's quarters in the main building to clean-up. After washing the blood out of her hair, the stationmaster's wife, Mrs. Harding, ran her a bath, and Elspeth soaked for twenty minutes, taking the opportunity to ponder on what had happened. Matron had been right, Mr. Spooner had been right. If she hadn't been there when Dr. Rogers pulled the plug of steel from the wound, and reacted as quickly as she had maybe no-one would have been in a position to pinch the end of the artery and prevent the young man from bleeding to death. For the briefest of moments she had looked around at the other nurses standing at the table. They hadn't moved. Even the doctor seemed frozen, the tweezers holding the shrapnel motionless in the air. Only she had ignored the spray of blood and reached into the torn flesh, and found the artery immediately. She had felt the pressure of the heart pumping the soldier's life out of his body, and had stopped it. It was also her voice which quietly and firmly called for a clamp. Mr. Spooner's words echoed in her head,

> "It is highly likely and probable that you will find yourselves on your own at some point in a life or death situation, with little if any assistance. You may

> not be able to cope, but you will have to deal with that."

Well she hadn't been on her own that was true, there had been others there. But she had managed better than she ever thought she would. A feeling of personal satisfaction suddenly made her feel that the luxury of the bath was a bonus earned that day. She had been tested, and knew now she could cope.

Bathed, wearing a clean uniform, and with a cup of tea and a slice of Mrs. Harding's cake inside her, she returned to the train with a more confident step. As she did so, a convoy of Royal Army Service Corps lorries was approaching the outskirts of Dover having driven down from Chelsea Barracks in London. They had come to deliver their loads of anti-aircraft ammunition for the destroyers, and clear the military equipment piled high in the railway sidings at the Marine Station. In the last vehicle, cheeky Jack Mason was sitting in the passenger's seat smoking a cigarette, his feet on the dashboard, and telling Private 'Snowy'

White, the driver, about the pretty nurse he had met on a hospital train at Victoria.

Cicely reached Elspeth's bunk carrying a cup of tea. Shaking her gently she murmured,

"Wakey, wakey, Miss. Nightingale".

Elspeth opened her eyes slowly.

"What time is it?" she groaned.

"Midnight. You've had all of four hours sleep and you've got ten minutes to dress. Mr. Spooner's here. He wants to see you".

Elspeth took the cup of tea carefully and squinted at Cicely.

"It's too early for jokes", said Elspeth sipping the hot liquid, "but thanks for the tea."

"Who's joking? He's driven over from Ramsgate specially, now shift it".

Elspeth looked at Cicely carefully for a moment, and realised she meant it. Handing the cup quickly to her she struggled out of her bunk.

"Oh, Christ! Why? What have I done?"

Cicely grinned.

"Who knows? Doc Harvey has been with him for the last two hours, and Doc Rogers".

"I knew it!" exclaimed Elspeth. "I shouldn't have said what I did to Dr. Harvey. And I shouldn't have gone to bed with my hair wet. Look at it!"

Mr. Spooner was sitting at a table in the restaurant car with Marcus Harvey when Elspeth walked in. She had plastered down her hair with water so that her cap would fit, but at least her uniform was clean and Cicely's insistence she should put on a dab of lipstick made her feel more presentable.

Mr. Spooner spoke first. Standing up he held out his hand to shake hers,

"Well done, Nurse Breen. That young man, whose life you doubtless saved, has a lot to thank you for. Sit down please. Would you like some tea?"

Elspeth shook his hand and for a moment didn't know which part of his conversation to respond to first. It came out as,

"Thank you, yes, thank you, yes please". Doctor Harvey smiled and rose from the table.

"I'll get them", he said.

Elspeth still couldn't believe what she had been invited to do. It seemed that Dr. Harvey had got his way. There had been a noticeable falling-off in the numbers of seriously wounded as Wednesday evening wore on. When this had been questioned by the medical staff, it had been confirmed that many of the wounded, particularly stretcher cases, were being held in France. This had allowed a greater number of able-bodied troops to be embarked unencumbered by their wounded colleagues. There was justification in this as hospital ships were in attendance outside Dunkirk. But when one of these was attacked by German dive-bombers, and then another despite their obvious markings which should have ensured their safety, the pressure to evacuate the wounded grew more pressing. Dr. Harvey had contacted Mr. Spooner with a plan to go to Dunkirk. He would take a team of volunteer nurses and they would assist medical staff already there to prioritise the wounded, and get them back if at all possible. Mr. Spooner had given his consent. After all, there was no point in having medical staff in a hospital train without patients. They may as well go to where they were needed most. So Elspeth, on the strength of her cool-headed actions, had been temporarily promoted, and asked if she would like to lead the volunteers who were to accompany Marcus Harvey across the Channel.

Back in Poplar, Simon was woken by Ma tapping on his door.

"Seven o'clock, Simon", she called.

"Thanks, Ma", he answered.

For a moment he lay looking at the small window next to his bed. He always slept with it open, and as a slight breeze caught the curtain he glimpsed a sliver of blue sky. He also heard Mr. Bassing from next door coughing his way to the outside toilet. That was something else he'd got used to. The outside toilets, or 'privvies', were constructed in pairs back to back. Ma's privy backed on to the Bassing's, and it was a shock on his first morning at Ashton Street when he was using the toilet to hear Mr. Bassing entering his on the other side of the wall. There had been silence for a moment, then Mr. Bassing had introduced himself and they had had a ten minute conversation through the wall. It turned out that Mr. Bassing was a very regular visitor at seven every morning, so Simon was able to avoid the experience from then on. He smiled as he recollected it, then shot up in the bed as he realised what today was. Today he was going to Dunkirk! Almost whooping with excitement he scrambled out of bed. He poured the water from the jug into the bowl and began to wash and shave while making a mental note to telephone his parents from Blackfriars as soon as he arrived at work.

"Have you got everything?" Ma asked, as she finished cooking his breakfast.

Simon rinsed his washing bowl in the scullery sink and placed it next to his jug on the drainer. He turned to look at her. She was standing with her back to him so he couldn't see her face, but knew by her voice that something was wrong.

> "I think so. They've given us a list. The usual things like wash kit and a change of underwear, but we shouldn't be gone long".

She nodded her head, but didn't answer.

> "What's up, Ma?"

He moved towards her and put his hand on her shoulder. She was crying.

> "Hey, what's the problem?" he asked gently.

She sniffed and began to lift the fried bread out of the frying pan and on to his plate. She put the spatula back in to the pan and turned towards him. Looking at him with tears in her eyes she pulled herself up to her full five feet and said,

> "I'm proud of you. And I'm proud of my Sid and my boy Robby. But I wish

> God wouldn't keep sending my men down to the sea in ships".

At that point she broke down and buried her face in Simon's chest. With a sad smile Simon, proud to be considered one of 'her men', put his arms around her shoulders and held her while she sobbed.

Throughout the Thursday morning there was a steady stream of visitors to the pontoon at Blackfriars. As Simon and the rest of the crew loaded stores, the Chief of the London Fire Brigade amongst many others came down to wish them good luck, and the Brigade Chaplain led them in a prayer for their safe return. Towards the end of the afternoon, the River Pilot came aboard, and the *Massey Shaw* slipped her moorings and set out for the estuary. It wasn't only a compass that had been considered superfluous when the fire-boat had been designed. Even her navigation lights were fit only for river work, so she was forced to dock as night fell at Holehaven on Canvey Island where they received orders to call in at Southend Pier on Friday morning to see if they were still needed. Simon cursed his luck, and he and the rest of the crew spent a chilly night wondering whether or not they would make it across the Channel at all.

Elspeth picked the team with Dr. Harvey. Practically all the staff volunteered, and she chose Cicely, and two nurses from Guys, Deborah Stone and Rosemary Franklyn. Deborah was everything the rest of them weren't physically. She had impressed them all with her ability to pick a grown man off the floor when one inadvertently rolled out of his bunk on their second day. Almost six feet tall and extremely strong, she had a quiet gentle nature and was a consummate professional in her nursing skills. Rosemary was much older. Her husband, an RAF Navigator, had been killed in a bombing raid over Holland only weeks before. She'd insisted on being allowed to come along explaining that it was the best way to avenge her husband's death - by snatching wounded soldiers from German clutches, a sentiment which Marcus Harvey heartily agreed with. The fifth member of Elspeth's team was her idea. John Traynor had been indispensable to them throughout their stay in Dover, and Elspeth was convinced he would be even more so on their task in France. Dr. Harvey would have preferred five nurses, but he could see the sense in what she said, and John was in. He was ecstatic. At nineteen he would be facing a call to arms soon anyway, and this way he would have a lot to talk about when that day arrived.

Elspeth arranged for the girls to visit the Stationmaster's wife and use her bath, then they packed a few items of clothing and wrote their letters home. John disappeared to the Station Rest-Room for a shower, and re-appeared with a new Southern Railways uniform and two spare sweaters courtesy of the stores manager. There was no way he was going to war without a uniform of some description he declared.

Dr. Harvey met with a Royal Navy Surgeon Commander at Dover Castle in charge of the wounded troop evacuations, and they agreed that most of the wounded in Dunkirk itself would make it onto a rescue ship. The concern was for those men stuck at the assembly point of Bray Dunes, around eight miles along the coast from the harbour. The medical team would be transported to the harbour by a Destroyer to be met by a Major David Vassalo of the Army Medical Corps. They would then travel to the Dunes by any means provided and assist the medics there in preparing the wounded for evacuation from the beach. They would also take essential stores with them as Major Vassalo had almost run out of sutures, morphine and blood plasma. Dr. Harvey contacted the hospital in Dover to prepare four cold-boxes packed with the units of plasma which would be delivered to the quay by seven that evening in the 'vampire van', the soldiers' affectionate term for the blood transfusion vehicle. The Destroyer, the

Commander informed him, would be held at the quay until eight. Dr, Harvey checked his watch as he left the Commander's office. He had three hours before the ship sailed.

Meanwhile, on the quay Jack Mason and the rest of the Service Corps drivers were getting ready to leave. The ammunition had been delivered to the Royal Navy armoury and their vehicles filled with the discarded equipment collected from the port area. Throughout the day they were constantly amazed at the sheer numbers of soldiers who trooped off the ships and onto the trains. For a while the drivers had questioned the inability of so many men to stop the German army in its tracks. But as they managed to talk to one or two, they began to understand a little of what had gone wrong. Too little ammunition, being prevented from constructing defensive positions by the Belgians – until it was too late, no air cover of there own and relying on the French for armour. Some of the men, they discovered, hadn't eaten or slept in days. Then a funny thing happened to Jack. Sitting in the cab of his lorry he found himself growing angry. Not over the things he normally would, such as another man making a pass at a girlfriend of the moment, or being overcharged for a pint of beer, but a deeper, more pressing anger about the injustice of it all. The fury within him built up in waves. He looked at Snowy, who was sitting behind the steering wheel of the lorry half asleep, and decided he had to do something.

"I'm going for a walk!" he stated, and opened his door and jumped out.

Slamming the door behind him he could hear Snowy's protestations as he strode off towards the quay.

Elspeth and her team were standing next to the gangplank of the Destroyer. Dr. Harvey had rushed back to the train for his own medical bag leaving Elspeth to supervise the loading of the stores. The pile of boxes had grown considerably in the past three hours, and Elspeth could tell that the Naval Lieutenant in front of her was anxiously waiting to leave. Two sailors and John were working their way down the pile, but the narrow gangplank was making things difficult.

The Lieutenant had introduced himself to them with a perfunctory shake of the hand when they had arrived. She was looking at him more closely now. He was young she decided, no more than twenty five, but his eyes were blood-shot, and when he stopped smiling the skin on his face settled on his cheekbones to make him look ten years older. His hands were thin, the fingernails bitten to the quick, and he smelt of tobacco and alcohol. She knew exhaustion when she saw it, and it was a good job that Matron couldn't see him she thought. He'd be sent to bed immediately! She was smiling to herself at the thought when, suddenly, she was physically spun round and found herself looking into those eyes again.

"Hello you!" the smiling face said.

"What..?" she managed to blurt out before being led a couple of paces from the others.

> "What indeed", Jack echoed. "Where are you off to?"
>
> "We're going to Dunkirk. To help fetch the wounded back", she stammered,
>
> "But what are you doing here?"

Jack looked at her pretty face beginning to redden again, and decided this was his opportunity.

"I've been sent to help you".

They looked at each other for a moment, he grinning, she completely bewildered.

> "But who sent you?" she asked.
>
> "Sarge," he found himself saying.

Over her shoulder he could see the pile of boxes and the three men struggling, and the lie became almost too easy. After all, he was a master at thinking on his feet. He went on,

> "They knew you would be having trouble with your stuff so they sent me to help. After all, we've been with you since London, 'aint we?"

"Yes. Oh, that's great. Does Doctor Harvey know?"

"If they've bothered to tell him. You know what the army's like. This is an emergency, so they're more than likely working on a need to know basis. And I'm just a gash hand. Is he in charge, then?"

"Yes, but I'm in charge of the nurses. I know, came as a shock to me too", she said almost apologetically.

"And no one better if I'm any judge. Well now you've got a soldier on your team as well. And speaking of which, I'd better earn me keep. Let me at those boxes. Don't want the Sarge chewing me up again, do we?"

Jack strode to the pile of boxes and with a wink in her direction, grabbed one in each hand and started down the gangplank. Elspeth watched as John recognised him and when, after exchanging a few words, they both burst out laughing a smile crossed her face. The trip suddenly had taken on a lighter note. It would be good to have him along.

The nurses were in the ship's wardroom by the time Dr. Harvey returned. He joined them as the ship began to shudder. Their host was the ship's medical officer, Sub-Lieutenant O'Shea.

"Call me Paddy", he had instructed them with a smile, then at their looks of alarm at the shuddering,

"It's only the old girl shoving off. Now, anyone for cocoa?"

They had all said yes when Dr. Harvey walked over to Elspeth.

"You got those stores on quickly, nurse. Well done".

"We were sent some help", she replied nodding in the direction of Jack who was talking to John and Cicely.

"Oh? Isn't he the chap who loaded the train in London?" he asked.

"Yes. The army sent him to help us. Wasn't that thoughtful?"

"Yes. But how did they know?" said Marcus suspiciously.

"They've been here all the time. I expect we've been too busy to notice. But he certainly made the difference tonight".

"I'd better welcome him to the team, then", he said, and walked over to Jack.

Jack saw him coming and came to attention.

"Good evening, sir", he said.

"Yes, good evening..."

"Private Mason, sir, sent to help you with your lifting and carrying".

"Yes, thanks. I'm sure we could use all the help we can get".

"You're right there Mr. Harvey," said John. "With Jack, we did the job in half the time".

"Good, though somebody might have informed me."

He was interrupted by Paddy entering the wardroom with steaming mugs of cocoa on a tray, and the announcement,

"Come and get it before it gets cold."

With thanks they all took a mug and were about to start drinking when Paddy went to a cupboard and took out a bottle of whisky. He grinned at them,

> "You'd all better have a tot of this to keep the cold out. Can't drink cocoa myself without it anyway".

As laughter filled the wardroom, Elspeth looked across at Jack. He raised his mug to her, and smiled.

After the cocoa, and another tot each of whisky, the captain of the Destroyer, Commander Dalkeith, came down to wish them luck. They were then taken to the ship's stores and issued with a life-jacket each. There was some alcohol-fuelled giggling from Deborah as she attempted to squeeze into hers, and Elspeth made a mental note to keep her away from any more whisky after she ended up on the floor with the hapless storeman trapped beneath her.

He had gallantly offered to help just as the ship lurched throwing them all off-balance. Paddy took Dr. Harvey and Jack on deck to show them the lifeboat they would need to use in an emergency, leaving the rest of them to settle in the wardroom and rest until the ship completed the crossing. Cicely parked herself in the armchair next to Elspeth.

"O.K. Els, what's going on?"

Elspeth sighed and opened her eyes.

"What?" she asked.

She was too tired to start one of Cicely's in-depth discussions. Paddy had said they would be at least four hours at sea, three of them avoiding mines, which hadn't exactly been welcome news. But it did guarantee them some uninterrupted free time, mines apart, so she had been looking forward to a nap.

> "This soldier boy", Cicely persisted. "Why has he suddenly shown up?"
>
> "I don't know, Sis. He said he'd been sent to help us, with the stores".

Cicely watched Elspeth relax back into the armchair and close her eyes again.

> "Well if you ask me it sounds mighty strange. Doctor Harvey seems to think so too", she went on, "judging by the looks he keeps giving him. Christ knows how he ended up here from London. Do you think he followed us down? He's obviously taken a shine to you. He's probably done a runner. If he has they could shoot him for desertion. Just think, some poor deluded bloke being shot because he fancied someone. I shouldn't want that on my conscience. How would you feel then?"

She looked for a reaction from Elspeth, but got none. Elspeth was asleep. Cicely looked around the wardroom. They were all asleep.

> "How can you sleep at a time like this?" she said quietly to no one in particular.

Turning on her side she closed her eyes. Within seconds, she had joined them.

Chapter 5

The Destroyer anchored half a mile offshore, midway between Bray Dunes and Dunkirk harbour at 1.00 o'clock in the morning. It had been a fairly event-free trip apart from nearly running down a Fishing Smack off the Goodwin Sands, just one of the dozens of small craft that had passed them in the night heading for England. Commander Dalkeith had cursed silently. The traffic was becoming worse than Regent Street the day before Christmas he declared loudly to everyone on the ship's bridge. But he had other things on his mind as he gave the command to drop anchor. The First Lieutenant, Philip Weston, was going to have to go ashore again to supervise the loading of the ship's lifeboats, and he knew that the man had little more to give. On his last trip, Weston had had to draw his pistol to prevent a determined group of soldiers from rushing one of the boats. They would certainly have capsized it. And that had been? The Commander pondered for a moment. Less than twelve hours ago. Nobody on the ship had slept for two days, which wasn't so bad when on board. But on the beach itself, facing down desperate men? No wonder Weston was at his wits end. Pulling men off the beaches was also a slow and laborious way of embarking the troops, but the harbour mole was full at the moment with a two hour wait to get in. It was time he couldn't waste. He gave the order for the lifeboats to be launched and went below to find this doctor and his gaggle of nurses. They wouldn't be able to leave the Destroyer until first light, but they could prepare their stores for off-loading in the meantime. It was all bloody nonsense anyway, he said to himself. The evacuation couldn't last more than a couple more days, and what were they expecting to accomplish in that time?

The girls were woken at 4 o'clock by Paddy and a sailor carrying trays on which was a bowl of porridge for each of them, and more hot chocolate. After a quick wash they assembled in their life-jackets to go up on deck. Dr. Harvey had decided to let the girls sleep when he had been woken by Commander Dalkeith earlier. Jack and John had loaded the Destroyer's launch as it sat on the deck, while Dr. Harvey was briefed by Philip Weston on what to expect once they landed. They would be put ashore in the harbour itself at 5 o'clock, by which time with any luck the Destroyer should be able to follow them in to the mole to finish loading. If Major Vassalo had managed to get his transport for them into Dunkirk, there would be a good chance they could get out to Bray Dunes. If for some reason he hadn't, then they had little chance of moving out of the town. The Destroyer had not been able to raise Major Vassalo since the previous afternoon to confirm the pre-arranged time-table. The launch would return for them on Sunday morning at around the same time. The obvious uncertainty in the plan, the survival of the Destroyer through the next forty-eight hours, was glossed over by the Lieutenant. If the launch wasn't there on

Sunday, they would have to get back as best they could. He then asked Dr. Harvey if he still wanted to be put ashore. The doctor thought hard for a moment. It was awkward not knowing if the transport would be waiting for them, but they had come to try and save lives, something few of the thousands of men crowding the town and beaches were qualified to do. The important word, he decided, was 'try'. They could at least do that. So he had declined the First Lieutenant's offer to return to England.

The medical team were seated in the launch as it was swung out and over the side. Elspeth was sitting between Deborah and Dr. Harvey. Directly opposite her, Cicely grabbed hold of Jack's arm as the launch bumped gently against the Destroyer's side on its way down. She grinned at Elspeth who narrowed her eyes at her. There was no need to enjoy the moment quite that much she glowered.

The ship had filled up throughout the preceding four hours as dozens of smaller boats and the Destroyer's lifeboats ferried the troops out from the beach areas. Not being able to use the launch had annoyed Commander Dalkeith. However, when it was time for them to leave he came down to wish them good luck, mollified somewhat by the absence of any enemy planes, so far, that morning. The embarkation had gone well, and he reminded the sailors manning the launch that they might make a late lunch in Dover, if they returned promptly.

The launch began its run to the harbour. The girls had been speechless when they first came on deck and saw the coastline and town. Dawn was trying to break but a pall of black smoke from a thousand fires was hanging over everything. The most oppressive was the smoke from the burning oil tanks on the edge of the town. It was thick and rolled skyward before settling into a layer which obscured the first light of the new day. But it was the mess the girls could see in the distance along the coast which made them gasp. They could actually see the soldiers on the beach, drawn up in lines which stretched from the sand dunes down across the beach to the sea. They could also make out scores of vehicles abandoned on the beach and in the dunes. Some had been driven into the sea and formed makeshift piers from which men were clambering into boats. Here and there a sunken ship rested on the sea bed, its superstructure towering over smaller boats ferrying soldiers to other ships including their own. The state of the men they had seen in Dover now made complete sense.

The launch approached a narrow wooden pier structure which towered above them and stretched from the town out to sea. The sailor steering the launch leant forward to talk to Dr. Harvey,

"That's the Mole, sir. We have to go around it and up into the harbour".

It must have been half a mile long. The lattice-work of huge timber beams sunk into the sea-bed looked substantial enough until the launch rounded the end and they saw clearly for the first time the row of big ships moored to it on the harbour side. The narrow structure was crowded with troops shuffling slowly along with men clambering aboard each ship in turn as quickly as they could. Dr. Harvey could see why they had been sent ahead in the launch. The traffic on the mole was strictly one way – out. He could also appreciate how awkward it would have been to move stretcher cases along it and still maintain the flow of men. Sailing this close to these big ships, their launch seemed insignificant and fragile, and a number of sunken ships lying on the harbour bottom with their damaged superstructures blackened and abandoned made them all realise how difficult the navy's job must have been in the past days. In the face of the enormity of what he was witnessing, Dr. Harvey began to doubt the sense of his determination to make this trip at all.

Major Vassalo was there. They could see him standing on the quay, hands on hips, framed by a backdrop of damaged buildings which had once fronted the marina road, some still burning from earlier air raids. The boats which would once have been tied in neat rows were away on the beaches helping the evacuation. As they approached the stone steps the sailor put the launch into reverse and brought it to a stop. A second sailor jumped ashore and began securing it to the landing stage at the foot of the steps. Major Vassalo turned and called to a small lorry sitting on the road, and two soldiers left it to run to join him on the quayside. The sailors began helping the nurses ashore while Jack and John started loading the boxes onto the landing stage.

Dr. Harvey ran up the stairs as Major Vassalo instructed his men to go down and help with the unloading. He arrived at the top and extended a hand to the Major,

"Major Vassalo?" he enquired.

"Good to see you doctor. Call me David", the Major answered shaking the proffered hand.

"And I'm Marcus, Marcus Harvey. Didn't know whether you'd make it or not. The place looks a terrible mess".

"Yes, sorry to leave you a bit in the air overnight. Terrible radio 'coms' from our beach hut. Still, you're a sight for sore eyes, and the stores you've brought, absolutely critical now. Shall we go and give them a hand?"

It was more of an order than a request, thought Marcus, as he followed the Major down the steps. But suddenly he lost his earlier feelings of doubt. In Major Vassalo he realised he had found another Mr. Spooner, a military surgeon at the top of his game, and seemingly impervious to the carnage of war all around them. The only niggle in the back of his mind was the thought that the stores might be a little more important to the Major than his own small team.

With the help of the sailors, the lorry was loaded quickly and they settled into the back of it for their journey through the destruction that was Dunkirk to the beach at Bray Dunes. Elspeth checked her watch. It was a quarter to six. What would the coming day bring, she wondered.

The *Massey Shaw* left Holehaven at first light on Friday morning to travel to the pier at Southend as instructed. They arrived at 7 o'clock, and the crew spent an anxious time while the Coxswain went with the pilot to the Customs Office at the end of the pier deck. After an hour of waiting the general consensus was that the evacuation had finished, and they had missed it. Simon found that thought impossible to bear and decided to go below into the cabin and make a pot of tea. He'd just lit the gas ring when he heard the sound of raised voices. Rushing out of the cabin he looked up to the pier deck where the Coxswain was striding back to the boat followed by another man in a blue uniform and tan duffle coat. The Coxswain had given the thumbs-up to the crew. The stranger was a Channel pilot. They were going!

Hugging the Kent coastline it took longer to travel to Ramsgate than first thought. They entered the harbour after mid-day and had to queue behind a line of fishing boats loaded with rescued troops before they could berth and report-in. It was their first sight of the troops snatched hours earlier from France, and it shocked them. The men looked all-in. Some were partly clothed, all looked dirty and unshaven. Most had managed to keep their weapons Simon noticed, but their obvious pleasure at being home was subdued. They were, after all, a defeated army. The victory, if there was one, was the navy's. Simon smiled and waved at a group sitting on a small fishing boat waiting to dock. They seemed too embarrassed to acknowledge his gesture.

When they eventually managed to thread their way to the harbour wall it was already one o'clock in the afternoon. While the Coxswain and Pilot went to find the Commander in charge, two Royal Navy sailors walked up to began filling the boat's fuel tanks. They clamped an anti-static line to the metal rail of the boat and wheeled out the diesel hose. Simon stepped ashore and stood watching them. Once the pump was switched on and the diesel flowing, one of the sailors turned to Simon.

"What you up for then mate?" he asked.
Simon considered the question for the briefest of moments before answering,

> "Fire-fighting, least that's what they told us".

Then he stopped, and looked at the fire-boat. With a grin the sailor spoke aloud what Simon was suddenly thinking,

> "Fire fighting? Bit late, 'ain't ya? I'd let the bugger burn".

With a shake of his head he went back to his re-fuelling. At that moment a naval Lieutenant came out and instructed them to load enough food for two days, and to sign for a large rowing boat. This was on top of a pile of others stacked on the quayside, and it took all of them to lift it down and launch it into the harbour. By the time it was securely tied to the *Massey Shaw*'s stern and they had located the food store and loaded provisions, the Coxswain was back accompanied by a Royal Navy Sub-Lieutenant, Tom Shepherd. He brought with him a steel helmet, pistol and a chart showing the location of minefields in the Channel from the North Goodwin Lightship to their destination in France, a distance of around 35 miles on Route X. It was probably as well for everyone's peace of mind that the issue of the compass's accuracy was completely over-looked in their haste to get on with the job. With the wind freshening from the east, and the sea becoming ever more 'choppy', they left at 3 o'clock, their destination - the beach otherwise known as Bray Dunes.

Matron had been so wrong about sandcastles and paddling, Cicely thought. By the middle of the afternoon she, Rosemary and Deborah had accompanied forty seven stretcher cases from the building being used as a medical centre in the dunes to the edge of the sea. Here they were carefully loaded with their stretchers lying across the width of the lifeboats sent from a Dutch coaster anchored out at sea. With six stretcher cases and eight walking wounded in each, the four separate lifeboats were tied in a line and towed out by a cabin cruiser, itself loaded with non-wounded soldiers. A sailor in each of the lifeboats took care of the steering. The nurses then trudged back up the beach with the medical orderlies who carried empty stretchers returned from the destroyer. The system was working well, but the 'to-ing and fro-ing' was beginning to wear the girls down. The sea had become quite rough, and Cicely had been completely soaked handing up an intravenous-drip bottle to a wounded soldier on the lifeboat for him to hold for the trip to the ship. The problem they all agreed was the height of the lifeboat's sides above the water. It was here that Deborah came into her own. As they had witnessed back in Dover, she was as strong as some, and taller than most of the orderlies, and her ability engendered a competitive edge among the men. But lifting soldiers on stretchers above the head while knee deep in a rough sea was taking its toll. That was the paddling. The sandcastles turned out to be wonderful feats of construction.

On most of the days since the previous weekend, the troops gathering on the beaches had been attacked by German planes dropping bombs or strafing with machine gun fire. Although this had caused casualties, they had not been as great as first feared. The fact that the sand in the dunes and on the beaches absorbed most of the blast from the explosions saved hundreds of lives. So the waiting men had constructed their own shelters in the dunes by digging-out caves and using lorry sand-channels, cab doors and body sides as roofs. It was into a state-of-the-art variation of one of these shelters that the girls had been shown when they had arrived earlier that morning.

The journey from Dunkirk had been slow

and bumpy. The small lorry, driven by David Vassalo himself, with Marcus next to him in the cab, wound around collapsed buildings and abandoned vehicles which littered the road out of the town. When they reached the village of Malo on the outskirts of Dunkirk they had to drive into a field to skirt a bomb crater which had obliterated the main road. At Leffrinckoucke a mile further on the Major slowed to be identified at a military checkpoint. Marcus realised how well known the man driving the lorry was when the Military Police waved him through with a cheery;

"Good luck, Doc!"

From this point on Marcus could see the dunes forming high banks on the left, and the road had been kept reasonably clear. The vehicles and guns of the British army were stacked in the fields on either side of the road, and Marcus could see groups of soldiers working among them.

> "What are they doing?" he asked the Major.

"Immobilising", the Major replied without looking.

Marcus gazed at the scene and wondered, how would Britain ever replace the acres of vehicles and equipment he was now watching being destroyed to stop it being of any use to the enemy?

They arrived at a small hamlet, pretty and seemingly untouched in the grey of the morning, and once through it, the Major began slowing down. He turned off onto a sandy lane running into the dunes and, reaching behind him to move the canvas curtain screen at the rear of the cab, shouted to those in the back;

"Hold tight. We're nearly there".

The lorry crawled along the lane between high hills of sand covered in marram grass for around a quarter of a mile, then turned a corner and there was the beach and the sea. The only building was a square blockhouse structure, single storey about the size of a detached house. It was covered in advertising boards and had a concreted parking area to the side nearest the track.

"Here we are", announced the Major.

"Gaston's Café and beach bar, or for us, home sweet home"

Marcus's team climbed out of the truck and stood and looked in amazement at the view in

front of them. As far as they could see the beach was covered in men. Most were in groups standing waiting their turn to walk out into the sea and board one of the small boats which were bobbing in the surf. Out at sea they could see the larger ships. As well as men there were vehicles of all sizes on the beach. In the shelter of some they could see more small plumes of smoke showing where breakfasts were being cooked when there was food, or water boiled. Along the edge of the sand the dunes rose quite sharply and in the valleys between, more groups of men and more camp fires.

After being unloaded by the medical orderlies, the lorry was reversed into a depression between two dunes twenty yards up the track from the building. It was roofed with a camouflage net, and half a dozen orderlies ran back up the track pulling a bundle of cut gorse bushes along the wheel-marks the lorry had made coming in.

> "Can't be too careful," said the Major.
> "they can see fresh tyre tracks from further up than they fly when they're trying to kill you."

He then took Marcus's group into the building to show them where they would be working.

The bar and café seating had been converted into a reception and preparation area. Two army medics and four orderlies were working on at least twenty casualties as the group filed through. The manager's office now had an operating theatre table set up in it, and eight Tilley lamps had been hung from the ceiling for light. The windows were boarded-up and covered with heavy curtains to hide any light at night. The kitchen was still fully functioning, but with the addition of a surgical autoclave in one corner. It also doubled as a dispensary. Major Vassalo opened the door of a large refrigerator to show them his depleted stock of blood plasma, which an orderly began augmenting with that brought by Marcus. With a nod of agreement from the Major, Elspeth put Rosemary in charge of this area immediately so that she could oversee the reception of the new pharmaceutical stocks. The last room must have once been a storage room. It ran the length of the building and was around nine feet wide. Now it held ten iron beds in a row in two of which were casualties who had undergone an operation in the night.

After a tour of the make-shift hospital the

girls were taken across the track to an enormous dune. It was here that they saw the largest sand castle of them all. Two lorries carrying mobile office bodies had been driven tightly next to the dune. A layer of sand had then been shovelled on top of their roofs from the top of the dune. Someone had even gone to the trouble of dragging vegetation onto the disturbed sand to camouflage the whole thing. The previous occupants, the Army Medical Corps staff, had been moved out of one that morning so that the nurses could stay in it until they left. Marcus was invited to move in with Major Vassalo, who was living in the rear of the lorry they had come down in. John and Jack were directed to a dune nearby which had been excavated already, and given tools to construct a bed each out of wood from a pile of packing cases. As well as their beds, over the next forty-eight hours Jack made scores of light-weight stretchers from lorry canvas covers and camouflage-net poles, and designed a floating stretcher mounted on two lorry inner-tubes.

Apart from Rosemary in the dispensary, there was little for the nurses to do immediately apart from move in to their accommodation. This soon changed dramatically. The first sign was a general movement on the beach. Then they heard shouting and watched as hundreds of men began running for the dunes, or dropping to lie on the beach. For a moment the nurses stood wondering what was going on, until one of the medical orderlies told them to get inside the office bodies straight away. German planes had been spotted heading towards the beach. They had just settled down inside and closed the door when a series of explosions followed. Cicely counted them aloud, five in total, about three seconds apart, and quite far away. There was a silence, and Cicely smiled nervously at Elspeth, then she screamed as an enormous explosion rocked their shelter, raining sand down on to them through cracks in the roof. Four more followed moving further away north towards the main road. Elspeth held on to Cicely who was trembling, her eyes screwed shut. They huddled for what seemed like hours, and then the door of the office body was opened and Jack poked his head in.

> "Everyone all right?" he asked.
>
> "No we're bloody not," sobbed Cicely, "I've wet my knickers!"
>
> "Well I'd change them," said Jack, grinning, "the boss wants you toot sweet."

Elspeth led her nurses out to begin a day that would last until after dark that night, and see over a hundred stretcher cases evacuated, around twice the previous daily average from this part of the beach.

Marcus and Major Vassalo worked non-stop in their small operating theatre. Bones were set, shrapnel removed, limbs amputated and two men died on the operating table. But ten more who would have, if their wounds had not received prompt attention, lived. As the last emergency case was carried out, the Major looked at his young assistant and said;

> "I'm impressed, doctor. You've a quick and safe pair of hands".

Marcus pulled his face mask down and smiled. This was praise indeed from a man who had successfully completed dozens of extraordinary surgical procedures in the past fourteen hours.

> "Thank you sir", he replied,
>
> "And may I say it's been a privilege watching you. I've learnt so much".
>
> "Nice of you to say, but piffle old boy. If you hadn't been assisting, I couldn't have done half the number we did. And please, cease with the sir. The name is David."

As they removed their surgical gowns and moved to leave the room, the Major turned to Marcus.

> "Those lasses of yours are good too. Nurses like those must be hard to find, particularly that tall blonde girl..?"
>
> "Nurse Breen", prompted Marcus.
>
> "Yes, Nurse Breen, she was damn useful, especially with that smashed

131

chest. Most lassies would have faded clean away. I'm impressed".

"I'll let her know", said Marcus. "You're right. It's partly because of her that we came here. A conversation we had back in Dover".

He smiled and went on,

"Now, I brought a bottle of Scotch with me..."

Chapter 6

An hour after leaving Ramsgate the crew of the fire-boat knew they had a problem. While still in sight of England, Sub-Lieutenant Tom Shepherd had discovered the fault in the compass. It gave a rough guide only, but by now they could see the smoke cloud hanging over Dunkirk, and the shallow draught of the boat meant that they should be able to slip over the sand bars beneath the water, so they carried on. The mines, however, continued to be a danger. The boat's steel hull meant it was as susceptible as the largest warship to being blown out of the water if it strayed too close to the magnetic variety, quite apart from the constant danger of running into one of the contact type. Another factor identified by Tom was that although they could get to Dunkirk following the pall of smoke over the town, no such landmark existed over the English shoreline, and they would be travelling blind after darkness fell. This had become particularly important when the crew were informed by the Coxswain that they would not be putting out fires after all, they would be rescuing troops from the beaches, and transporting them back to Dover. As they powered on through a worsening sea, the motion of the boat began to have an effect on the crew. Quite simply, the *Massey Shaw* was an appalling sea-boat, her flat bottom and length meant she pitched and heaved at the smallest wave. Sea-sickness soon claimed the first victim which acted like a trigger, and before long four more men were being violently sick. Simon tried to take his mind off the awful sensation in his stomach by counting the columns of small boats they had begun to pass. These were the cabin cruisers and motor yachts being towed by fishing Drifters and tugs from many ports, similar to those he had seen two days before on the river. Then at around 5 o'clock there was something else to hold his attention. It was impossible to hear much above the noise from the *Massey Shaw*'s engines, but he could see them in the sky over the distant French coast. He counted thirty aeroplanes flying in a rough formation. Making his way to the 'dodger' where Tom was talking to the Coxswain, he tapped Tom's arm, and pointed to the planes. Tom lifted his binoculars and watched for a moment before handing them to Simon. For the first time Simon saw the German Luftwaffe in action. The planes appeared to be bombing the town. Within hours, the *Massey Shaw* would share the experience.

They came in sight of the beaches in the late afternoon, and like Elspeth and the medical team they were shocked. The sheer numbers of men on the beach, and in lines in the sea had them gazing in disbelief at the enormity of the task. Two large warships and an armoured trawler were anchored about half a mile out to sea with a constant stream of small boats ferrying men to them. After avoiding the funnels and superstructures of two larger vessels sunk further out, the Coxswain manoeuvred the boat between the overloaded cabin cruisers and lifeboats making this journey, and crept in closer to the shoreline. The bow of the boat grated on the sea-bottom and the Coxswain quickly reversed into slightly deeper water before dropping anchor. As the boat's engines stopped they could hear the shouts of men above the noise of the sea breaking on the beach.

The crew wasted no time, and two climbed into the rowing boat they had towed from Dover and rowed the thirty metres towards the nearest line of soldiers waiting in the water. They were standing waist deep, the surf lifting to the level of their chests at regular intervals. Simon and the rest of the crew watched as the rowing boat approached to within a few feet of them, and the two firemen called to the soldiers to wade out a little further, one at a time. After some hesitation, a half a dozen rushed the rowing boat and, despite protests from the firemen, tried to haul themselves into the boat all at once. In horror the crew watched the rowing boat capsize leaving the soldiers and firemen floundering in four feet of water. Fortunately they were able to struggle to a small motor boat that had just arrived, and were eventually transferred to the *Massey Shaw*. They now had eight soaking wet men on board, but no rowing boat to enable them to get any more. All around them the

water was littered with pieces of wreckage and small boats manoeuvring around obstacles on their way out to the larger ships. Men were shouting and occasionally there would be the noise of explosions from distant German artillery. The fact that the beach areas and even ships lying at anchor were now in range of some of the advancing German guns added a heightened sense of anxiety to the operation. Men were becoming desperate for their own salvation and among the stoic patience of the majority the fire-boat crew were to witness some disturbing examples of isolated selfish behaviour that proved at the least embarrassing, and at worst dangerous to soldier and rescuer alike.

Firstly though they needed another small boat to take the place of the one sunk earlier. There was an RAF launch grounded on the shoreline filled with men who, worried in case they lost their place aboard, would not get out in order for it to be re-floated. Tom decided to try and haul it off the beach using the fire-boat's powerful engines. After two unsuccessful attempts to fire a line on to it by small rocket maroons, Tom and Simon shed their protective clothing and swam to it. Unloading the soldiers on board, who only retreated to the beach after being promised a swift return once the launch was freed, they tied the line then dropped into the water to help push it off. As it gradually began to float, the soldiers were suddenly joined by their friends who had been watching from the beach, and around thirty men waded through the water and clambered aboard. The launch's bow bottomed on the sea floor once more under their weight, and Simon and Tom cursed as the line went tight, then snapped half way along its length. Without the line to secure it, the stern of the launch suddenly swung round side-on to the waves, narrowly missing Simon, and in its top-heavy state rolled over, throwing the soldiers back into the shallow water which poured into it as it settled on its side on the sea floor. Simon waded out to join Tom on the beach and together they walked off in disgust, leaving the soldiers cursing wildly as they tried in vain to right the water-filled vessel.

It was 11 o'clock before a suitable boat was found. They had walked for a mile in the direction of Dunkirk stumbling over wreckage, and on one occasion, two dead soldiers, whose bodies were revealed by the ebbing tide weighed down to the sea-floor by their heavy equipment. They had argued with soldiers who thought they were trying to push-in a queue, and then Simon had the luck to fall into the back of a half-sunken lorry. As he floundered around inside he realised that he was standing in a small dinghy which after a lot of struggling they were just able to turn and manhandle out onto the beach. Tom realised that the sea had receded considerably, and when high tide returned, the lorry would be many feet under water. It was this that must have kept the boat hidden from others scavenging like them for a means of escape. Now all they had to do was find the *Massey Shaw* out in the darkness, and hang on to the dinghy. They were going to need help.

Cicely had fallen asleep over her food in the kitchen of the cafe medical centre. Despite being shaken and prodded she refused to wake, so Deborah carried her out into the night and laid her to rest in the office body. Rosemary stayed on in the dispensary as there was still the odd wounded soldier turning up who needed attention, but Marcus insisted that Elspeth join the other two nurses and get some rest. They had all tasted Marcus's whisky, Elspeth making sure that Deborah ate first. But she need not have worried. Deborah knew the importance of the operation, and there would not be a recurrence of the incident on the destroyer while she was working.

Jack Mason and little John had astounded them all. Apart from Jack's light-weight stretchers they had been making, and the floating stretcher idea, John came up with an ingenious plan to help get those stretchers down to the sea for evacuation. The medical orderlies had carried dozens of men to the water's edge, which became a major hike as low tide drew the rescue boats further away from the cafe medical centre, and by mid-day some had been showing signs of collapse. John had been helping them leaving Jack to work on his stretchers when he hit on the idea. Grabbing a small sack, he filled it with packets of cigarettes from the café storeroom and wandered off into the dunes. Here he quietly looked for small groups of men, one or more of whom had to be tall, then approached them with a proposition. If they would agree to be co-opted as temporary orderlies, he would give them three packets of cigarettes each, and by them carrying a stretcher, allow them the opportunity of moving nearer a rescue boat. In an hour he had a score of men signed-up to his plan. By 10 o'clock that night, all but four of the 'volunteer' bearers had managed to get away with the wounded, the four having agreed to stay with the medics until the next day. When Major Vassalo found out later he was so impressed at this remarkable display of initiative he invited John to contact him when he returned to England and finished by telling him,

"My unit could use a man like you".

It was the first time such praise and recognition had been handed out to him, and was the more gratifying coming from such an obvious professional like the Major. Later, curled up in his dug-out in the sand, John dreamt of saving the wounded from a hundred battles into the future, and smiled in his sleep.

After cutting a decent roll of canvas from a three-ton lorry body, Jack was trudging his way to the same dug-out when he saw the white figure in the darkness. Elspeth was sitting on the wall which bounded the entrance to the café looking out to sea. Putting the canvas down Jack made his way quietly across the sand towards her.

"You do this a lot?" he asked.

"Oh, Jack!" said Elspeth turning quickly, "you scare a body to death".

He laughed and sat next to her.

"You'd be no good on guard duty".

She gave him a wry smile and nodded,

"You're right, I'm too much of a dreamer. Anyway, what do you mean, what am I doing?"

"Sitting", he said simply, "on your own. You always seem to be on your own".

She turned her head to look back out to sea.

"I like that sometimes," she answered.

He lit a cigarette, carefully cupping the match flame in his hand, and they sat quietly for a moment. The sea was almost at low tide and the whoosh of the surf was muffled and distant. There were still the odd calls of men out there in the darkness, but the explosions which had formed a backdrop of sound all day had died away.

"This reminds me of Wells", she said, breaking the silence.

"What, Somerset?" he replied.

"No, Norfolk. It was where we used to go on holiday as children".

"They have lots of wrecked ships and machine guns there, then?"

He grinned and shrunk from her slap on his arm.

> "Of course not", she said, then rubbed his arm. "Sorry, I'm not usually that violent".

She went on,

> "You mock Wells-next-the-Sea at your peril. It was a yearly pilgrimage for all us kids. Gillying, that's catching crabs on a line to you, watching ships load grain at the wharf, then off to Old Hunstanton for lunch in the Strange Arms, sheer bliss. And the sea there goes out easily as far as it does here".

Jack looked at her. Her white uniform reflected what little light there was onto her face and blonde hair. Gently he took her chin in his hand and turned her face to him.

"You are truly beautiful", he said.

And for once in his life, Jack meant it as he leaned forward to kiss her.

Tom and Simon found the help they needed, an orderly column of infantry waiting patiently for the next small boat to appear. Tom went up to their officer and explained their predicament. In another five minutes he was signalling with the officer's torch out into the darkness. A couple of minutes more and they could hear the *Massey Shaw*'s diesel engines and a hail from the boat. Simon shouted back and, with four of the soldiers, Tom rushed off to fetch the dinghy. When they returned, these four and two others, using planks from a wooden box, paddled the dinghy off into the darkness. The dinghy was paddled back by two of the firemen towing another rope with them. This was secured to an abandoned lorry further up the beach and the evacuation began, each dinghy-full of men hauling themselves back to the fireboat with one staying on the dinghy to haul back to the beach. This was made easier by the tide turning. They had four hours to get the men off before the incoming tide covered the lorry. With the help of the officer they did it in two, and the *Massey Shaw* weighed anchor with so many men on board that the sea was frighteningly close to the deck at the stern. At the wheel, Andy May eased open the throttles and gently the boat set off smoothly into the darkness for Ramsgate. Standing in front of the compass, Tom turned slightly to Simon, and with a wry grin held up crossed fingers.

As the *Massey Shaw* set-off for home Elspeth was quietly opening the door to the office-body shelter. With a trembling hand she closed it and felt her way to her camp bed lying next to the left-hand wall. She couldn't quite believe what they had just done. Sod it, she thought struggling to undo the buttons on her nurse's uniform. It should not have been like that the first time, or any time. The old cliché that life was too short to worry offered her no comfort at this moment. She certainly didn't need this sudden complication in her life. Why couldn't he have just left her to sit in peace having a quiet think? She folded the grubby uniform and dropped it onto the floor, then lowered herself gingerly onto the bed. With a slight grimace she eased the blanket over herself and pushed off each of her shoes. I'll have to clean myself up in the morning she thought and within seconds was asleep. Six feet away in the dark, Deborah closed her eyes again, and went back to listening to Cicely snoring softly in the camp bed next to hers.

The boat's engines had been roaring below for an hour when Tom suddenly tapped Andy on the shoulder.

"Slow down a minute!" Tom shouted.
Andy reached for the throttle levers and pulled them back. Immediately the boat settled into the water and the bow wave disappeared.

"What's wrong?" Andy asked.

"I thought I heard a plane", said Tom. He scanned the blackness behind them.

"What, over the noise we're making?" questioned Andy.

"There's something", said Tom, "and the phosphorescence at the bow and in our wake will shine like a beacon from up there".

Andy poked his head from behind the canvas dodger as Simon squeezed his way past the soldiers to join them.

"Trouble?" asked Simon.

"Tom thinks we've got company", replied Andy, who went on with a grin, "I just hope they don't want a lift, we've got no room".

There was a sudden huge explosion about a hundred metres behind, and as they instinctively ducked the boat heaved into the air. Spray rained down on them accompanied by shouts from some of the men on board as the sea lapped over the stern.

"Jesus!" exclaimed Andy.

"Go forward slowly, and bear off to port a bit", Tom instructed.

Andy pushed the throttles forward slightly and spun the wheel to the left.

"Not too much!" shouted Tom.

Andy slowed the boat a fraction until it was just moving forward, hardly disturbing the sea's surface. It was the bane of all covert military sea activity. Phosphorescence, the light given off by plankton in disturbed sea water, had already proved fatal to other boats on the Channel crossing that week. But Tom was aware of its importance, especially at this time of year. He called for silence as the men became restless. The men quietened and they all heard it, circling off to their right. Andy settled himself behind the dodger again and waited for Tom's instructions.

"All stop!" Tom said.

Andy cut the engines completely, and in the silence they heard the plane begin to dive. It came in from behind along the track they had been travelling a few minutes earlier.

"Brace yourselves!" shouted Tom.

They heard the whistling noise of the bomb just before it hit two hundred metres from the first, still close enough to rain water onto them. The boat rocked violently, and men clung on as the shock waves hit the side.

"At least they can't see us", Tom said,
"They're guessing. Thank God it's still dark".

For five minutes everyone remained still while the plane searched for any tell-tale sign of their position. Then, on the horizon, an enormous flash lit-up the sky. Seconds after the flash had subsided to a glow, they heard the boom of the explosion.

"Oh, my God!" exclaimed Andy. "What in the world was that?"

"Probably a mine", Tom answered quietly.

"That?" Andy spat, "That's a mine? And there's us with a knackered compass!"

But the fate of the unknown vessel accomplished one thing in their favour. It drew the plane away. Andy summed-up their thoughts as he started the boat's engines and continued on their way,

"I expect they've gone to bomb the survivors!" he raged.

There were no further incidents and The *Massey Shaw* pulled into Ramsgate harbour at 7 o'clock on the Saturday morning. Sixty five cold and wet soldiers disembarked, most of whom had been sea-sick on the journey. Some had been so crammed in that they had to be helped ashore, but the discomfort and perils of the journey were soon forgotten with the relief and joy of being home. While the soldiers were led away for whatever breakfast they could face, the boat's crew began cleaning it ready for another crossing.

The nurses awoke to the sound of an aeroplane screaming low over the café. As they lay on their camp beds they could hear the distant shouting of men on the beach, and the futile gesture of machine guns being fired at the attacking planes. Cicely stuck her fingers in her ears and shut her eyes, while Deborah reached over to give her a comforting cuddle. Rosemary stirred, sat up, then went back to sleep. Elspeth watched them in a detached way. She had other things on her mind. What was she going to do about Jack? After last night he was bound to think there was something between them. There obviously was now, but not what he was hoping for. She had succumbed to the wave of sympathy that washed over her as he told of his fears in the past and hopes for the future. A childhood comprised of miserable poverty, followed by the salvation of the army, thrown away on a whim by joining them on this journey, and why? Because, he said, he couldn't resist her when he saw her on the quay in Dover. She had been tired last night, but that was no excuse. No, not even if the 'tired' was really exhausted. And no woman's first experience of making love should have been like that, in the dark, on a beach, and in a war zone, for Christ's sake! Elspeth made her decision. There was a job to do, and more deserving souls than Jack were relying on her to do it. He would have to wait. She wouldn't tell anyone that he was not supposed to be here, after all, he had worked hard to help them save lives, but she couldn't help him with his problems – not yet anyway. She checked her watch. It was half past seven, time to face another day.

In Ramsgate there had been a meeting. Tom decided that a naval shore party would be more useful on the beach loading operation, so the decision had been made that only four of the firemen would go back to Bray Dunes. This was a relief to one or two, but the others took some convincing. It was finally agreed that Andy, Simon and two of the Auxiliary firemen who had been engine mechanics before volunteering for the fire service should go. It was a fortuitous decision to include them, they would be crucial later. Six armed naval ratings made up the shore party under Tom's command. When the boat had been cleaned-out and re-fuelled, the firemen went for their breakfast, and those returning to Dunkirk tried to grab an hour's rest. A new thirty foot rowing boat was found and secured behind the *Massey Shaw* and in the middle of the afternoon she set off for France again.

Chapter 7

The inside of Gaston's Beach Café and Bar was packed with wounded soldiers. Many had been making their way towards the town along the beaches and had been caught in the open by the increasing level of artillery fire. It was obvious to everyone that the German's push at the perimeter defences, throwing everything at a last ditch attempt to wipe-out the British and French forces, was beginning to tell on the defenders somewhere in the fields beyond the beaches. In the middle of the morning a messenger had made the perilous road journey from Dunkirk to inform Major Vassalo that the evacuation was likely to end early the next morning, Sunday. Elspeth had been shocked when she was told. Not that the evacuation was ending, but that it was Saturday, only a week since her last night-shift at St. Thomas's. It seemed like a lifetime away, and in some respects it was. Certainly she would never be the same person again,

> "I always knew I should have been a vet", she confided to Rosemary.

Rosemary on the other hand was both elated and disappointed at the same time. By tirelessly administering to the wounded, she felt some of the pain of losing her husband ease - she'd thumbed her nose at the Germans. But she was sad that they would of necessity have to leave before all the wounded could reach them.

> "I could hang on here", she suggested to Marcus. "I've nothing much to get home for after all".

He had turned on her with a coldness borne out of tiredness and a deep sense of responsibility for his nurses.

> "And that would achieve precisely nothing", he'd said dismissively.

Elspeth saw the agony of frustration in his eyes. The same thought as Rosemary's had occurred to him while he lay trying to sleep the night before. How could anyone abandon the wounded? But he also realised that being taken prisoner would not help the thousands who would need his and Rosemary's skills over the coming.., and at that point he was forced to stop. Who knew how long before this war would end. That was the true terror.

Elspeth had not seen much of Jack. They had all grabbed a frugal breakfast of biscuits and powdered milk, as rations were diminishing at an alarming rate, and David Vassalo insisted that those wounded who could eat would have something. Jack had just finished his when she managed to break-off from assisting the doctors in the operating room. As they passed each other he'd given her a smile and a wink, then left to prepare more stretchers. She wondered as she sat down if the smile and the wink were somehow linked. Maybe he wasn't the 'cheeky chappie' after all. It could be just a facial tic. She smiled to herself at the thought, and abandoned the idea. He was cheeky alright, and impossible to say no to. She ate her 'mushy' biscuit to the sound of approaching planes, lots of them, and was amazed at how calm she felt.

Out on the beach men were once again looking for cover. Little John was nearly out of cigarettes, but had enlisted the help of fifteen British soldiers and, with the aid of an English speaker amongst them, six French. These were the first French soldiers he'd seen. He stayed talking to them for a while and witnessed the approach of the planes.

"Stukas!" shouted one of the soldiers. They all crouched down in the dune, but this time the bombers ignored the beach. John counted forty of them as, like seagulls, they began diving on a group of warships a couple of miles out. He could see the black puffs of smoke from the warship's anti-aircraft guns which were followed by the 'pom-pom' noise which had become so familiar to them over the last two days. Then there was a flash, and a boom, as a bomb struck home. Seconds later, one of the planes pulled-up hard trailing smoke,

"They've got the bastard!"

The shout was from someone in a nearby dune, and they all began cheering. All that was, except John. He crouched there with tears welling in his eyes watching the dual out at sea. It was the unfairness of it, forty harbingers of death onto three or four victims. His emotions tore him back to childhood experiences where not having a father and being the smallest in his year at school had exposed him to unfairness like that. The relentlessness of such attacks by bullies had bred in him a resourcefulness that people like Major Vassalo now valued, but had been developed at enormous personal cost. He slipped away quietly to make his way back to the café.

Around mid-day, David Vassalo and Marcus stepped outside the café for a cigarette. David stretched then rubbed his neck.

"I'm getting too old for this", he said, then laughed, "What am I talking about?" he went on, "I wonder what the age limit is for battlefield surgery".

Marcus smiled and joined in the banter,

"Or even cafe surgery".

"Something to boast about in Harley Street though", he went on.

"I shall never get there, old man. Couldn't live with all that money, it would spoil me", David replied, grinning.

They stood for a moment smoking and listening to the gunfire in the distance.

"What time do you want to start the pull-out?" asked Marcus.

"Hadn't really settled on a plan", replied David, "how many stretcher cases are there now?"

"Seven at the moment. The orderlies got fifteen away at first light, and John's rounded up twenty or so helpers for this afternoon".

"He's a good chap, that John", said David.

"Yes, and Private Mason. I don't know what we would have done without them", Marcus added.

"I agree", replied David, "he'll be good company in the camp, Private Mason. And that John, I offered him a job with me once he's called up. Shame I'll have to let him down".

Marcus flicked his cigarette end into the sand and gave Major Vassalo a questioning look,

"I'm not sure I follow", he said.

"I'm staying on, and Private Mason has volunteered to stay with me. Actually he approached me this morning. He'd guessed I couldn't leave now, and said he'd like to stay and help".

There was a silence while Marcus digested this staggering news. It was obviously catching, this staying behind thing,

"I'd no idea.. I'm stunned. Do you think that's wise?" he said finally.

"Come, come, old man. You'll have to leave the military decisions to us military types. It's one of the few perks we've got."

He paused,

> "Sorry, that sounded patronising, and I didn't mean.."

Looking at a crestfallen Marcus he smiled and, patting him on the shoulder said,

> "I know. It sounds ungrateful of me, but you have to go back. Get those young ladies of yours home to civilisation, they'll be wasted here, in some camp, especially that Nurse Breen, eh? You tell her from me to train as a doctor, any sort will do, she'll be good – mark my words".

He turned to walk back to the café,

> "Better get on. I want to get that Frenchman's leg off before tea. And then we'll discuss getting you out. Better leave it until the early hours though. It'll be safer, and anyway, you've a boat arranged for first thing tomorrow don't forget".

Jack had just finished cutting the canvas from the back of a lorry when John walked up to him. He saw the pain in John's eyes and frowned.

"What's up, Titch?" he asked.

"I've run out of fags", he replied.

Jack could see the hurt was deeper than a lack of cigarettes, but decided not to pursue it.

"You can give me a hand with this, then. It's the last for miles".

John looked along the beach. Jack was right. For as far as he could see there were lorries littered around, all with no canvas covers. He brightened up suddenly with his admiration for this particular accomplishment.

"Bloody hell, Jack!" he exclaimed, "How many stretchers you made?"

"I dunno. Fifty, sixty maybe. But I ran out of poles first thing. I'm using bundles of radio aerials now. Trouble is they bend a bit. And I'm getting low on lacing string. Still, I hear we won't need many more".

> "Oh? How's that then?" asked John, as he reached up to take the roll of canvas.
>
> "'Tween you and me, and don't say nothing to the others, we're pulling out sometime tonight or early tomorrow. Job's done evidently".

Jack jumped down onto the sand and picked up an end of the canvas. John lifted the other and they started back along the beach.

> "Can't say I'm sorry, Jack. I've really enjoyed your company if you don't mind me saying, but it'll be good to get home, and I'll be proud to buy you a pint in the first pub we come to, how's that?"
>
> "I'll look forward to it, Titch. For sure, I'll do that and no mistake".

For the briefest of moments Jack was glad John was walking behind him as another unfamiliar emotion welled inside. He had grown really fond of this chirpy little person, barely a man, who asked nothing of anyone, but with a glad heart endeavoured to help everyone. He wished he'd met him sooner, wished he'd met them all sooner, especially Elspeth. He had forgotten how many times he'd used a girl in the past, how easily an innocent could be charmed by him into surrendering her modesty. But never before had he experienced the choking strangeness he felt at the mere thought of her now. The compulsion to just stand and watch her was overwhelming. He was in love.

It was the middle of the afternoon when the orderly on the radio finally managed to reach the headquarters of the British army in Dunkirk. He reported the reply to a grim-faced Major Vassalo, who didn't need telling that conditions were now critical. All the beaches east of Bray had been abandoned, including the British HQ at La Panne, and this last area of sand was under constant bombardment by German guns. The defences manned by only a few thousand British troops and remnants of the French XVI and III Corps were barely managing to hold the Germans who, at their closest, were only three miles away on the opposite bank of the Bergeus-Furness Canal. Most of the soldiers destined for evacuation were making their way to the harbour in Dunkirk where a last desperate effort was under way to save them from capture. The reply had been brief. Get out by Sunday morning at the latest.

There had been a lessening in the numbers of wounded reaching the café throughout the day. Men were still turning up with wounds which were treated, after which they were pointed towards the road and told to get to town. Boats continued taking others off the beaches, but the danger from artillery fire and plane attack had increased so much that the dunes were rapidly emptying as men were directed to Dunkirk. Marcus and Rosemary were busy tending the dozen casualties that lay on stretchers in the back of the café, and Cicely and Deborah were bandaging the wounds of a group of French soldiers when Elspeth managed to take a break. Marcus had told her to prepare her nurses for the trip home and she wanted to speak to Jack in private.

Walking down towards the shoreline she could see Jack in the distance helping to lift a stretcher onto the deck of a cabin cruiser. It was obvious even from here that the other three men with him were French. Unlike most of the British soldiers, the French always seemed to have their strangely shaped helmets on. Deborah had made them laugh the evening before when they were talking about that very thing suggesting, unkindly, it was to hide their strangely shaped heads. Elspeth stopped and watched the French soldiers drag themselves aboard the cabin cruiser, an effort not helped by their insistence on also always wearing their heavy greatcoats as well. Sodden with water they must have been enormously heavy she thought. Jack steadied the small boat to prevent the stretcher from sliding off as the soldiers almost pulled it over, then pushed the bow out until he was chest deep in the sea.

With a wave to the sailor steering it he turned and made his way back to the water's edge where, for a moment, he dropped to his knees to recover from his exertions. The tide was reaching its highest point and small waves were breaking over his legs. Then he gave a start and half rolled over as something bumped into him. Elspeth watched as he turned in the water, and reached forward to grab hold of whatever it was. As he stumbled to stand up, what she saw made her gasp, her hands flying to her mouth. Jack was struggling to pull the body of a soldier by his webbing straps out of the shallows and onto the beach. After he had pulled the dead man above the high-water mark he sank down on his bottom and looked at the body for a moment. Elspeth watched with tears streaming down her cheeks, as he slowly leaned forward and gently ruffled the dead soldier's hair before lying back on the sand, his fore-arm across his face. She realised that anything she had to say to this man who could display such tenderness would hurt him too deeply now, so she turned and made her way back to the café. They could talk once they were out of this madness.

Andy steered the boat as closely as he could to the beach in the gloom. It took all his skill to avoid the broken vehicles and sunken wreckage that was now exposed at low tide. It was dusk, but there was enough light to see that the beach was dramatically emptier than it had been the night before. With smoke clouding the edge of the water, Andy searched for a safe place to drop the sailors of the landing party. He made his choice, an area of clear water between two half-sunken fishing boats, and dropped anchor. The landing party boarded the rowing boat and pulled for the shore where they set-up a small marshalling area. Then they began the slow process of rounding up and ferrying the waiting soldiers out in the rowing boat.

With scores of packed men on board, the Massey Shaw carefully made her way to a troopship lying a half a mile out, transferring the cold and wet soldiers despite the heavy swell. But as she returned to the beach for a second load, the port engine began to misfire, and finally stopped. With only the one engine Andy struggled to get the boat into the original position, but finally made it and dropped anchor again. Now the decision to send the two mechanics as crew paid off, and while the rowing boat began its shuttle service to and from the beach, they disappeared below with torches to find out what had gone wrong with the engine.

The nurses had packed their meagre belongings and were ready to leave. Marcus had tried once more to change David's mind about staying. But with two seriously injured men who couldn't be moved, and only three units of blood plasma to share between both, David knew that he would have to monitor them closely and besides, as he quipped,

> "Can't stand sea crossings anyway, and I could do with a rest".

The last six serious casualties had been loaded onto the last of Jack's stretchers, and they were only waiting for a suitable boat to appear when John came rushing in with the news that there was one. He had spotted it as it was leaving with its fourth load and had stayed around to find out if it would come back. He realised it would when the group of sailors it had brought with it stayed on the beach. So he'd asked them to hang on as they had some wounded to get off, then run back to tell the medical team.

"And you'll never guess", he said grinning, "it's a fire engine".

Cicely, who was bandaging a French soldier's leg, mumbled through the safety pin held between her teeth,

"What, with a ladder?"

"No, it is! It's a fire-boat, from London".

Elspeth suddenly realised what he'd said, and turned to him,

"Are you serious?" she asked.

"'Course I am. It's from the Thames. Good old London town!"

At that moment Jack walked in with the last of the group of soldiers recruited earlier by John to act as stretcher-bearers.

> "There's a boat that's ideal for the stretchers turned up, some fire-float or something. Are we ready? Could be our last chance."

He looked at them all, then more closely at Elspeth. Her face was bright red and she looked as though she was about to cry. He started towards her, concern in his eyes, but was stopped by Deborah who gave him a knowing look and a barely perceptible shake of her head.

> "Come on then, let's get them aboard", Deborah ordered quickly.

The room was suddenly all action as the stretcher cases were carried from the long room at the back, through the café, and outside onto the beach. Jack fussed around them, seeing them safely through the front door.

> "Watch those handles! Don't bounce too much, they'll bend".

Major Vassalo appeared from the kitchen with

the last of Marcus's whisky in a small tumbler,

"It's got busy, problems?" he asked.

Jack came to a half-hearted attention and told him,

> "We've a boat for the last of the stretcher cases. Just taking them down now, sir".

The Major turned to go back to the kitchen. Over his shoulder he said,

> "Well done, Mason, well done".

As the last of the stretcher cases left the café, Elspeth grabbed John.

> "Did you find out the name?" she asked.
>
> "Name?" he said laughing, "What name?"
>
> "Of the boat, the fire-boat", she replied, impatience creeping into her voice.
>
> "No. Didn't know they had names. Don't they have numbers?"

He looked puzzled as if this was another mystery he ought to solve,

"Why?" he asked.

Elspeth suddenly gave up. She thought of the young man she had met so briefly. When was that now? Oh yes, a lifetime ago, before her world had become an insane rush of bloody and broken bodies, dirty clothes and dead men floating in the sea. It doesn't matter, she thought, but found herself saying lamely,

> "Oh, no particular reason, I've got a friend in one, that's all".
>
> "I'll find out for you", he volunteered.
>
> "No, you're all right, John. It would be too much of a coincidence anyway".

Cicely stood up and smiled at her French soldier, then patted his bottom. As he grinned at her she growled at him,

> "Asseyez-vous!"

He sat down looking sheepish.

Wiping her hands on her smock hem Cicely walked over to John,

> "The boat's name is *Massey Shaw* and the bloke's name is Simon. Els couldn't stop talking about him in

Dover, and only met him the once. Got to be love at first sight!" she said.

"Great!" said John, his face lighting up, "*Massey Shaw* and Simon. I'll go and find out if your bloke's on it right now", and he rushed off outside.

Cicely frowned as Elspeth gave her a despairing look.

"What?" Cicely asked innocently.

Following Elspeth's glance she turned her head to look over her shoulder. Jack was standing in the doorway of the long room. His face betrayed the shock that Cicely's announcement had brought. Then, with a wry smile, he made his way past them to the front door where he paused and turned. Looking at Elspeth he said,

"Everything's tickety-boo back there. Good luck, and think about me sometimes".

He winked at her and disappeared into the night, almost bumping into Marcus who had returned from loading the lorry that would take them to Dunkirk. Sensing an atmosphere as soon as he was in the room, but totally misinterpreted the reason for it, Marcus said,

> "I know ladies, it is hard to leave under these circumstances".

Elspeth strode past him towards the door and he called after her,

> "It's two-thirty! We're off at three!"

In the darkness the *Massey Shaw* was on her way back to collect another load of men. The engine was working fine now, an air lock in the fuel filter had been bled, and sea water drained from a sediment bowl. John had questioned each of the sailors, and, although they knew the name of the boat, none of them knew the names of the firemen on board. He was now waiting for the boat to anchor so he could find out from its crew. Deciding he needed to pee, he walked off to go behind a wrecked lorry and had just reached it when the scream of an incoming artillery barrage sent everyone racing for cover. The men waiting for the boat dropped to the ground, joined quickly by the stretcher-bearers who had run the last ten metres to get off the open expanse of sand. Explosions pounded the beach and the water's edge, and the fire-boat was deluged in spray containing pieces of wreckage and body parts of drowned men.

The barrage ended as quickly as it had begun. At the edge of the water Jack eased himself to his feet to begin overseeing the loading of the first three stretchers and their bearers. Once the rowing boat was full he waded along its side to the first sailor on an oar and shouted up at him,

"Is there a fireman called Simon on that boat?"

"Dunno mate", came the terse reply.

Jack's hand shot up and grasped the sailor's wrist. With blazing eyes he snarled,

"Well find out! Mate!"

Jack spat out the word 'mate', and threw the sailor backwards off-balance. The sailor recovered his position and looked down on the angry soldier glaring up at him, and decided not to argue. The moment was broken by Tom shouting from the shore,

"Shove off".

The sailors leaned into their oars and began rowing out to the fire-boat, and Jack waded ashore. For a moment he watched the rowing boat, then turned to survey the beach. There was no sign of John.

Even though it was night there was still enough light to make out groups of mainly French soldiers who were dotted along the shoreline waiting for their turn in the boats. They were concentrated now at the western-most end of the beach, nearest the town and furthest away from the direction of the German shelling. Jack began walking towards them, but he stopped as he heard a faint call. Turning, he waited to hear it again, but the tide was coming in. All he could hear was the surf beginning to break on the beach. Then he spotted a movement. Something was moving next to a wrecked lorry further up the beach from the *Massey Shaw's* landing party. He heard the cry again. It was coming from that direction. He jogged back and past the stretchers on the sand. There was only one group of men further on, being crammed into a fishing boat. He noticed they were using a ladder to clamber out of chest high water and into the boat, and made a mental note that this was a good idea, should they ever have to do this again! The lorry was in line with the group, about thirty metres in from the sea. He walked towards it calling.

"Titch! Are you about?"

There was a momentary pause, and Jack saw the movement in the gloom at the same time as he heard the call,

"Over here, Jack! By the truck!"

John was lying next to the lorry waving the only piece of canvas left on the beach, and Jack was running to him before he finished shouting.

Jack dropped onto the sand beside him.

"What's up, Titch?"

John half grinned at him then nodded towards his legs which were under the truck. Jack reached down and slid them out. John moaned and lay back on the sand. His right foot was missing. Jack's immediate reaction was to duck down to see if he could find it, but the sight of a darker patch of sand growing at the point of the leg where the foot should have been concentrated his mind. He had to stop the bleeding. He took off his shirt and ripped the two sleeves from it. He tied one tightly around John's thigh just above the knee, then looked around for something to use as a tourniquet. His eye fell on the wing mirror of the truck. Jumping up he went to the door and tore the mirror from its mounting bar. Wrenching the bar up and down he broke it off and rushed back to John.

"I'm cold", John moaned.

"So am I", joked Jack, "and you've ruined my shirt".

John smiled then let out a yell as Jack, using the mirror bar, wound the shirt sleeve tightly on his leg. Ignoring the yell, Jack used the other sleeve to tie the bar in position, then stood before bending down to pick him up.

"You see," he said, "all that medic training, it did pay off".

But John had passed-out. Jack picked his small body up and began trotting back to the group at the water's edge.

The rowing boat had just reached the shore as Jack ran up. He splashed into the sea and lifted John up out of the water towards the sailors inside. They reached down and took him, passing him to the back of the boat. Jack grabbed the side of the boat and shouted,

"Look after him, he's my friend! Oh, and tell someone he's got a tourniquet on! Right?"

The sailor Jack had grabbed before looked over the side and said quietly,

"O.K, we'll watch out for him".

There was a movement from the bow of the boat and Simon jumped into the water to wade to the sand. Once there he waited for Jack to reach the edge of the water before going up to him,

"Are you looking for Simon?"

Jack stared at him for a moment before answering him with a question.

"Is your boat the *Massey Shaw*?"

"Yes", replied Simon, "and I'm Simon, Simon Parson. Do you know me?"

Jack looked him up and down and a smile crept across his lips,

"You'd better be good, boy. No, I don't know you, but I..."

He was cut short by the sound of the scream from another barrage of German shells heading towards them. Simon saw the expression on Jack's face change instantly to fear, and as men began to throw themselves to the sand, he stood rooted with indecision. His arms came up to defend himself as Jack grabbed him by the shirt and pushed him down on the beach. The first shell exploded metres behind them showering them with debris, and Jack pressed Simon into the sand. Crushed beneath him, Simon began to struggle to escape. Jack held him for a moment, but when he wouldn't stop, lifted himself slightly and punched him hard on the edge of his jaw. Stunned, Simon lay still as more explosions rocked the beach. There was a grunt from the man lying on him, and the weight pressed down even harder. Simon could feel a stabbing pain in his chest but couldn't move.

After a few brief seconds the barrage was over. Simon regained his senses and tried to move the man pinning him down. He managed to wriggle free and sat for a moment looking at Jack, face down and motionless on the sand. Simon grimaced with pain and looked at his own chest. He could see little, but when he touched the front of his shirt it was wet, with blood. He looked more closely at his 'attacker'. There was steam coming from his back. He bent forward to see what it was. A large piece of jagged metal was protruding slightly from the bare flesh. He reached to touch it then whipped his hand away quickly, his fingers singed by its heat. Simon rolled on his side and vomited, which caused him to cry out with the pain in his chest.

Tom had rushed over and was now kneeling by him,

> "Where are you hurt?" he asked.
>
> "It's my chest", gasped Simon, "but what about this chap?"

Tom rolled Jack over and looked at the gaping chest wound,

> "I'm afraid he's had it", he said. "Let's have a look at you".

As Simon sat back Tom opened his shirt and inspected his chest with his torch.

> "There's a few puncture marks, might be some shrapnel, but the blood seems to have come from your friend here. I think there's a medical unit up in the dunes if you want to go and get checked out.."

Simon shook his head,

> "No, I'll wait 'till we get back to Ramsgate. I don't want to hold things up. Are we nearly ready to shove off?"

Tom stood up and switched off his torch.

"Yes, only these last few stretcher-bearer bods to load. About ten minutes I should think. We've lifted around five hundred chaps tonight. I think that's a fair night's work. Oh, sorry, can you make it?" Tom asked.

He reached down to offer Simon a hand.

"Yes, thanks", Simon said as he grasped Tom's hand and struggled painfully to his feet.

Simon stood looking down at Jack's body,

"I thought he was attacking me. He slung me down and I couldn't move him off me! Do you know who he is?" he asked.

Tom looked at Jack, then at Simon and, after a pause said,

"It looks like he's the man who saved your life chum".

Chapter 8

February 28th 1946
Wells-Next-the-Sea, Norfolk

Holding on to each other and huddled against the bitter February wind blowing in off the North Sea, Elspeth and Cicely walked slowly along the beach road,

> "How could he want to come here for his birthday?" mumbled Cicely through the scarf she had wound around her mouth to keep out the cold, "its bloody freezing!"

Elspeth looked at her. The wind had dragged small tears from Cicely's eyes which sat on her cheeks. Elspeth laughed,

> "He's five, today, of course he wants to come to the sea-side. You're spoilt girl, too much sun. Wait until he wants an ice lolly. We'll all have to eat one, you know."

Cicely shuddered,

"No chance! He might be five, but, just think, if you'd waited another day 'till the 29th, he'd only be one, or is it two..? Anyway, we could be indoors changing his nappy, instead of.. God its cold!"

Elspeth patted Cicely's hand,

"Sis, stop moaning".

Smiling she went on,

"Don't you miss this, just occasionally?"

"No I don't!" Cicely replied, "Thank God I married Ted. California sun, California peaches, oranges, warm blue sea and sky. When was the last time you saw a peach?"

"Before those you brought with you last week, about ten years I should think", Elspeth replied.

"Exactly! And you could have had a Yank, don't you remember? And marrying so quickly, within a month Els! What is it, marry in haste, repent

> at leisure? Still, at least having a baby straight off tied him up. Sorry, that was tactless".

"Not at all", said Elspeth, still smiling at her, "We're very happy, thank you for asking and anyway, tact was never a strong point of yours – I'm glad to say".

Cicely hugged Elspeth's arm tighter, then looked behind her for a moment where her husband Ted was walking with Simon. They were in a deep conversation about something. She leaned in closer and said quietly,

> "He's better looking than Ted, I'll grant you that, but is he spoiling you?"

Elspeth laughed again before replying,

> "You mare! It's not all about money, but thanks for the compliment".

Cicely went on,

> "No I think Simon's great. He's so good at being a dad".

They walked on in silence for a few moments.

About fifty metres in front of them, Elspeth's mother and father were each holding a hand of their grandson who was skipping along between them. At intervals he would squeal in pleasure as they lifted him into the air. Cicely broke the silence,

> "Your mum and dad are great with him, Els".
>
> "They spend a lot of time with him, now I'm taking over dad's surgery", replied Elspeth.

She went on,

> "I've got my final exams next year, then it'll be Elspeth Parson, RCVS, Veterinary Surgeon. I can't wait. And Simon's up for the Commander's job at Peterborough".

Cicely hugged Elspeth's arm again and said,

> "Yes, I'm proud of you, Els. You don't miss nursing then?"
>
> "Sometimes, especially the friends. It can be a bit lonely on your own on a day like today with your arm up a

horse's how's-your-father, but I don't miss the misery, had too much of that, you know.."

Cicely looked sideways at her friend and said tentatively,

"Do you ever wonder what happened to him?"

Elspeth carried on walking. Only a slight hardening of her eyes betrayed the emotion the question had stirred in her.

"I know what happened to him", she stated.

Cicely looked at her questioningly,

"I thought nobody did", she ventured after a moment's hesitation.

"I do", said Elspeth. "He's here, with me. He's with me all the time".

Cicely's face softened,

"Of course he is, I understand", she said softly.

"No you don't, Sis. I'm not being philosophical, I mean it. He really is here with me. I'll show you".

Cicely dropped her arm as Elspeth reached inside her handbag and took out a small silver box.

> "You're never to tell anyone about this, Sis. If you do I will haunt you. Only Marcus Harvey and I know what's in this box, so promise me".

Taken aback by Elspeth's seriousness, Cicely giggled nervously.

> "No, I'm serious, Sis, promise", Elspeth insisted.

> "OK, I promise", Cicely answered.

Elspeth opened the box. On a small pad of cotton wool lay six pieces of bone, each around an inch long. Cicely looked at the fragments, then at Elspeth.

> "That's him?" Cicely asked incredulously.

> "Some of him", Elspeth replied.

> "Oh, Els, you're joking!" exclaimed Cicely.

Elspeth glanced over her shoulder. Simon and Ted were still a good way behind them deep in conversation, but she frowned at Cicely,

"Keep it down, Sis!"

Cicely suddenly looked shocked, and whispered intently,

"You're serious! But how..?"

Elspeth closed the box and replaced it in her bag, then took hold of Cicely's arm as they started walking again. Patting her hand she said,

> "You remember how Simon was brought in to St. Thomas's the day we got back?"
>
> "Yes, he'd collapsed or something, hadn't he?" said Cicely.
>
> "That's right, well it was Marcus who checked him over. Simon told him about the soldier with no shirt who covered him on the beach and saved his life, but was killed. Anyway, they operated thinking there was shrapnel in Simon's chest but found the bone fragments instead, and they weren't Simon's. The next day after they tidied-up little John's leg, John told

him all about how he was rescued and who by, and Marcus put two and two together and managed to retrieve these from the post-op bag. These belong to the man who saved Simon, the man with no shirt on because he'd used it as a tourniquet on John, the man with a piece of shrapnel in his back."

Cicely's eyes widened,

"But why did he give them to you?"

"Because he knew I was concerned about Jack. We'd talked about him on our way home from France, and he wanted to stop me from worrying. He thought it would be better I knew. When he told me what they'd found in Simon, I asked him to get them for me, which he did".

Cicely stopped walking for a moment and looked at her friend,

"So they're definitely.." she said.

Elspeth smiled at her,

"Yes. I know it sounds gruesome, but those bodies floating in the sea, Sis. How many would have been picked-up and given a decent funeral? And despite hanging on to these, I even kidded myself that he couldn't have been one of them. So I religiously checked the POW lists each year, but he was never on them. By last Christmas I knew for sure. But I can never tell Simon. And I don't want you telling Ted either. For his own peace of mind Simon must never find out."

They walked slowly arm in arm in silence for a minute, then Cicely said quietly,

"Thanks for sharing that Els. You can trust me with this one, and of course I won't say anything to Ted. But why is it so important Simon doesn't know?"

Elspeth stopped and looked at her,

"Because there are still some pieces inside Simon they couldn't move. He'll be part of Simon for ever, and I don't

> want Simon to have to live with that thought. It wouldn't be fair".

Cicely stood with her mouth open as Elspeth began walking after her parents who had stopped to let the others catch up. Their grandson let go of their hands and started running back towards his mother. Elspeth dropped to one knee and opened her arms as he reached her. She spun him round and up into the air. While they both laughed, Simon and Ted walked up behind them, and Elspeth handed the boy to Simon who held him to his chest and said,

> "Come on Jack, birthday boy, race you to Nanna and Granddad".

With a squeal of pleasure and a big grin on his face, the boy hugged Simon's neck and, looking over Simon's shoulder, winked at Cicely.

> "Oh, my God", Cicely breathed quietly to herself, "he *is* here, it's his ..!"

The End